THE BILLIONAIRE'S AUCTION

BRI BLACKWOOD

BRETAGEY PRESS

NOTE FROM THE AUTHOR

Hello!

Thank you for taking the time to read this book. The Billionaire's Auction is a dark billionaire enemies-to-lovers romance. It is not recommended for minors and contains situations that are dubious and could be triggering. The book also includes flashbacks to child abuse and sexual assault which might also be triggering. It isn't a standalone and the book ends in a cliffhanger. The next book in the series is The Billionaire's Possession.

BLURB

Desperate times lead to desperate measures...

That's how I ended up in an auction.

The money from it would be my way out.

My last chance.

Then I saw him, and hope flashed through my mind when he placed a bid.

It shouldn't have.

Because I didn't know about the dark edges that surrounded his soul, the ones that should never see the light of day.

Now I'm tied to him for ninety days, but I can survive this.

I've been through so much worse before.

Or so I thought.

Because my hope? Was nothing more than a façade.

Now, he was my monster.

PLAYLIST

Angel With A Shotgun - The Cab
Sine From Above - Lady Gaga, Elton John
Shivers - Ed Sheeran
You Ruin Me - The Veronicas
abcdefu - GAYLE
The Essence Of Me - Leona Lewis
When I'm Gone - Alesso, Katy Perry
traitor - Olivia Rodrigo
It'll Be Okay - Shawn Mendes

The playlist can be found on Spotify.

1

———

ACE

The candles flickering in the distance glowed as hushed whispers of the chant I knew by heart danced around me. Someone had placed the candles around the room for effect, not because it was necessary. The ceiling lights that would have normally lit the space were turned down low to give the illusion of a more mysterious, intimate setting.

This was all done to create the environment where we could perform our rituals and then move on to our business meeting before everything was brought to a close and we went our separate ways. The Chevaliers operated efficiently and effectively; they had done so for hundreds of years before us and would continue to do so once we all left this earth. The chapter at Brentson University fed into the Chevaliers headquarters in New York City because many of the members there ended up in the city after graduation.

Some of the richest and most influential men in the world belonged to the Chevaliers. We'd all taken an oath to support the good of this organization and in return, reaped the benefits of all, especially monetarily. It paid to be on the right side of the chairman's orders because the consequences would be deadly.

When the chairman's eyes met mine, his slight nod made me think of what I'd gone through to get to this point. Not everyone made it to initiation, no matter how much money they threw at the organization. In some cases, it had become survival of the fittest and the men in this room had won. We'd come out on top.

After going through several rounds of tests, I was initiated into the secret society with several friends who felt more like brothers. We'd seen some things that I could never unsee. But I was devoted to the organization for all that it had done for me. Quitting wasn't the easiest thing in the world. Once you were a member, the only way you left was in a body bag.

When the chanting stopped, the overhead lights brightened, making it easier to see everyone in the room. We didn't bother with cloaks, scepters, and some of the other apparatuses that some of the younger members used, but the symbolism and devotion to the organization was still alive and well in here.

As one walked down the hall before reaching this room, you could spend your time looking at some of the history of the Chevaliers. Historical exhibits and photos that featured our founders were scattered at various headquarters around the world.

When the business meeting started, I patiently waited as the current officers spoke about the latest news within the Chevaliers. As the meeting went on, I leaned on the arm of my chair with my head in my hand, my index finger landing on my temple.

"Bored?" the man next to me whispered to not disturb the report being given.

I glanced over at Kingston Cross but didn't change my body language. "No, I just have things on my mind."

"Like the meeting with Will?"

This time I shrugged but kept my attention on the man speaking in front of me. Kingston and I needed to talk to Will DePalma, a member of the Vitale crime family. He'd wanted Cross Sentinel, the security organization that Kingston founded, to do some investigating into an acquaintance for him, and Kingston passed it off to me, thinking that I would be perfect for the job. Deep down, I knew it was another attempt by Kingston to convince me to join his team. While I had no intentions of doing so right now, the thought was enticing. I had other matters to deal with and preferred to act alone.

Kingston wasn't the only person giving out assignments the day I'd met up with him at his girlfriend, Ellie's, apartment. I dropped a bombshell on him that he had a half-sister attending Brentson University, the same college we all attended and not too far away from my estate.

I was looking forward to that consultation more than this regular meeting of the Chevaliers. Lucky for me, both were scheduled for the same evening because I was only planning to spend one night in the city.

"Damien's going to tag along with us, if you don't mind."

Damien Cross raised an eyebrow at his cousin. "Tag along? You're awfully chatty today."

I smirked when Kingston didn't have a quick response. Damien was right. Kingston usually got straight to the point, more fixated on observing the people around us versus small talk. In fact, he was taking more after his cousin, Gage Cross.

Damien, Kingston, and I were initiated into the Chevaliers in different years, but our connection to the organization built a camaraderie among its members, or so it tried. Anyone would be lucky to have the Cross family on speed dial.

The Cross family were an instrumental part of New York City and the state. Their power in the city was extraordinary and being connected to them opened doors. But being that my grandfather finally acknowledged me when I was a senior in high school helped too. After all, he needed to make sure that the heir to his real estate dynasty was properly trained for the role. It, of course, led to a shitshow, but in the end, I had leverage from the prestige of my family name as well.

I adjusted myself in my chair as I concentrated on the speech being given in the front of the room. My eyes floated between all the men in the room, as this was a conference among some of the richest men in this country. Wheeling and dealing were done within these walls, and most of it would never be known to the public.

The current chairman of the Chevaliers, Parker Townsend, stood up and said, "As this meeting is coming to a close, I wanted to invite you all to Brentson University in a few weeks to attend initiation. Details will be sent at a later date."

There were a few more closing announcements and the session ended. Before I could blink, Parker had walked over to where I was and stuck his hand out to greet me. "It's been a while."

That was true. I hadn't been to a meeting in person due to other business matters I needed to attend to.

"It happens. Is there anything I can do for you?"

Parker's and my social circles sometimes crossed, but we were more friendly acquaintances than friends.

"There's something I need to discuss with you, privately. Shall I leave a note with your secretary at your office?"

"Are you not going to give me a hint as to what this might pertain to?"

"It's something that I don't think either of us want disclosed in public."

I raised my eyebrow at him as I could feel Kingston's and Damien's stares.

"I'll be in touch." I watched as Parker walked away, greeting someone else that was standing a few feet away.

"What was that all about?" Kingston's question almost sounded far away, as if we weren't in the same room as one another.

"I'm not sure," I responded.

Silence sat between us momentarily before Damien changed the subject. "You know, this place has given folks a lot of business ideas over the years."

"So, this was how Elevate came to fruition?" I asked.

Elevate was a bar and sex club that Damien founded with his brothers. It was one of the hottest spots in New York City and the demand to attend, whether once or to become a recurrent customer, was through the roof.

"It wasn't the reason Elevate came about, but I won't deny that we have hosted a significant number of Chevaliers at our establishment."

This was a shock to no one. Given some of the activities

our fellow brothers had taken part in, I suspected that what happened at Elevate would be tamer than some things they were used to. It wasn't surprising that even outside of this clientele, Elevate was as successful as it was.

Instead of focusing on one of the many business ventures that the Cross family owned, I patiently waited for Damien and Kingston. I grabbed my briefcase and the three of us walked out of the building, avoiding small talk or chit-chat with anyone else in the room. We had somewhere important to be and understood the urgency of getting there.

"Rob can take us to Will's place," Damien said as we walked out of the back door and a dark SUV pulled up in front of us.

I'd left my car at the hotel I was staying at overnight, so I had no issues with taking Damien up on his offer. Before Rob could step out of the driver's seat, Damien opened the back door and allowed us to file in. Once we were seated, Rob pulled away from the curb.

"Hopefully Will has more information than what was in that file, because it was minimal at best," said Kingston.

"He's usually very thorough."

I looked at Damien out of the corner of my eye and said, "You seem to have a close relationship with him."

"Let's just say that our pasts are intertwined more than either one of us would prefer them to be."

"Trust me, I know that feeling."

A memory of how I was connected to Kiki Hastings flashed in my mind before I shoved it into the furthest corner of my brain. I was tempted to ask Damien what he'd meant, but now wasn't the time to dig through old wounds, especially when I didn't want to open mine.

The drive to Will's office was shorter than I'd expected, and before long, we were sitting in the chairs in front of his desk. His office reminded me of what I'd found when I'd walked into my grandfather's home, days before he announced that he was retiring and moving to his private island in the Caribbean. I had done little to change things since I'd moved in there, however.

"Welcome," Will said as he took a seat behind his enormous desk.

Anyone looking in on this meeting would think that Will was the one running this show, but I knew differently. I'd met Will on several occasions and recognized that his usual confidence was dimmed. I wondered if it had something to do with what was in the file that I'd just placed on his desk.

"I didn't expect you to join us, Damien."

"As you very well know, it's always a pleasure to be in your company, Will."

Will grunted. "I'm sure everyone in this room would agree with you. Anyway, let's cut to the chase. We need to talk about Falcone because I want this operation to begin now."

The urgency was clear in his voice and put me slightly on edge. I hadn't had any interactions with Clay Falcone, but I knew of some of the people that he had dealings with. Several of them were shady motherfuckers, but who was I to judge since I'd gotten an assignment from the Mafia? "Spill all that you know about him," I said.

"I assume Kingston showed you the file."

I nodded. I had read it over several times since Kingston had given it to me. "But I wanted you to tell me why you want me to get involved with Falcone and investigate his property and not, say, someone within your organization."

"I've known Falcone for a long time, and we've been cordial, but I got word that Jon Moretti was feeding information to him."

Damien spoke up. "Is that why you didn't have a huge issue with me killing him after he disrespected Anais?"

I studied both men, one by one, before my eyes landed back on Will. Damien killing one of Will's men could easily have caused a lot of bloodshed, and that was a risk he'd been willing to take to support the woman he loved.

"That's correct, even though I wish I would have gotten to him first."

"You have to be quicker than me," Damien said as he sat back in his chair with a smirk on his face.

Will looked at him for a long moment before he turned his attention to Kingston and me. "The leaks have continued, even though Jon is no longer among the living, and they are giving Falcone pertinent information about my businesses."

I knew that was code for more of his black market dealings.

"But you still haven't explained why one of your men couldn't look into Falcone."

Will ran a hand across his face. "Falcone will spot one of my men from a mile away, but he might be more willing to let someone who isn't connected to me in. In the end, he's motivated by money, and I want to know what he's doing at that estate. If he's encroaching on my territory after the agreement we made..."

Will didn't have to finish his sentence because everyone in the room knew what would happen.

"Understandable. I'm willing to do this under one condition."

"Name your price."

We both knew I didn't need his money, and I knew he'd pay me handsomely. "I get to do this my way, with no interference from anyone. I'll keep you informed about what I'm doing, and if I need anything, I'll let you know, but you don't get to direct this."

Will glanced out of his office window with New York City's skyline displayed before us all. "Fine. I want everything I can get to make Falcone understand that he's fucked with the wrong man."

2

———

ACE

I pulled open the front door of Bar 53 and walked inside. It had taken only a couple of days to get on Falcone's calendar, and I spent that time researching everything I could about him. For someone who was supposed to be conducting both legal and illegal businesses in New York, it was very easy to gather basic information about him. What I hadn't been able to find was what he was doing at the property Will wanted to know more about. That was even after doing a deep dive into what businesses he was running in general and watching the house like a hawk. I'd done enough homework on him to know that he was holding an event there in a few days and that I needed an invitation to attend.

As I studied Bar 53, taking account of anything noteworthy, a blonde woman standing behind the bar caught my attention.

"Sir, may I help you?"

I turned and found an overly eager host standing in front of me, several feet away from a podium.

"I'm here to see Clay Falcone."

I used his full name although Falcone would have been sufficient. He was well known by just his last name. It was easy to see when the moment my words registered with him because his eyes widened.

"Uh, yes. Let me just call down and announce your arrival."

He scurried back to the podium before grabbing a walkie-talkie. Either this guy was normally jumpy, or Falcone had instilled fear in him. Neither reason was enough for me to spend more than two seconds thinking about it.

A quick glance at my Rolex proved that I was a couple of minutes early. I found myself staring at the blonde who'd caught my attention as she served up another drink. Her long hair was hanging loose over her shoulders, and I fought the urge to run my fingers through it.

Although she tried to be coy, I'd seen her taking glimpses at me as I stood there waiting to be directed to my meeting with Falcone. When our eyes met, she averted her gaze first and stared down at the glasses in front of her.

I watched as the blonde moved effortlessly behind the bar as if she'd been doing it for all of her life. I didn't think that to be the case since she looked young, maybe in her early twenties, but I could have been wrong. Chances were I wasn't, but that was another reason to stop thinking about her. Focusing on Falcone would lead me to wrapping up this case faster, not thinking about how fast I could get one of his bartenders underneath me.

"Mr. Bolton."

I dragged my eyes away from the woman in question and turned my attention to the man who interrupted me. "Yes?"

He shifted his weight under my gaze. "My name is Ian and I'll be taking you to Mr. Falcone."

I let myself glance at the bartender once more before I followed Ian's lead. He took me to a set of stairs that led down into the basement. Why I needed to be escorted when it was easy to see that his office was the one with the guard standing in front of it was beyond me. Ian nodded at the security guard, and the guard knocked on the door. A muffled "Come in" announced that it was okay for us to enter.

The guard opened the door, and both Ian and I stepped into the office.

"Ace Bolton."

"Clay Falcone," I responded in kind.

He stood up to shake my hand before turning to Ian. "Thanks for showing him in. You may leave."

Ian dipped his head slightly before exiting the room. Falcone waited until the door shut before looking at me. "Sit down. Can I get you anything? Water, an alcoholic beverage?"

My mind briefly wandered to the beautiful bartender I'd seen just moments ago before trying to size up Falcone's game plan here. He wasn't known for his niceties, so this approach was interesting. "I'm good, thanks."

He turned and sat behind his desk, and in the seconds it took for him to do so, I'd written up a description of him in my head and scanned what I could see of a couple of papers that he'd left on his desk in plain sight. Outside of a few receipts from things I deemed related to the bar, there was nothing out of the ordinary.

"I was surprised that it took you this long to reach out to me."

"Oh?"

"I expected to hear from you soon after your grandfather retired. The mark he left on this city will never be forgotten, by the way."

He wasn't being sincere, and it had now been years since my grandfather had retired. Falcone and I didn't run with the same people, so I hadn't expected to hear from him, but I wasn't about the bullshit he was spewing.

"I'd prefer not to talk about my grandfather right now."

"Fair." He grabbed a glass that he'd had on his desk before I arrived and took a sip of its contents. "Rumor has it that you're trying to get into other lines of business."

So he'd done some research on me as well. Too bad I planted that story when I was doing some digging on him. "Depends on the offer at hand. I'm always looking to expand our influence in the best way possible."

"I work in many different industries, Mr. Bolton. I can open doors for you to make your bottom line even more lucrative."

"I'm intrigued. Tell me more."

The smile that crossed his lips would have been unnerving for many, but I stared at him while keeping my face blank, determined not to convey what I might be thinking.

"I can give you one better. Come to an event I'm having at one of my homes upstate. I think you'll be interested in the theme. That will give you a taste of what I have in mind."

I knew that he had two properties upstate that were public knowledge. I was getting closer. "When and where?"

"In a few days. The address will be on the invitation."

I didn't want to arouse suspicion by asking about the event. "I look forward to receiving it."

"You know, I'm glad you decided to pay me a visit this evening."

"Oh, yeah?"

Falcone was trying to size me up, determining whether I was worth his time. When a small smile appeared on his face, I knew that I wasn't going to like the next thing that came out of his mouth. "You and I aren't that much different, Mr. Bolton. We're always looking for the next business opportunity, the next high."

He and I weren't anything alike. Falcone had drawn that comparison up in his mind without knowing a damn thing about me.

"Plus, your grandfather and I had dealings as well, so I'm glad we can see if it's worth keeping the tradition alive."

That, I hadn't found in my search. Maybe there were some things that Falcone kept to himself. "What type of dealings did you have with my grandfather?"

"I'd rather show you than tell you. I have your address, and you should get something in the mail in a few days." His office phone rang on his desk. He looked over at it before looking back at me. "Now, if you'll excuse me, I have another matter to attend to."

I debated whether it was worth dragging this out further, not really giving a shit if I took up more of his time or not. It was clear that he knew some things that I didn't and was using it to entice another meeting between us.

But I refused to show any sign of weakness.

Instead, I stood up and held my hand out. "It was nice meeting you, Falcone."

He followed suit and gave me a firm handshake. I

returned the favor before he said, "Likewise. I assume that I will see you soon."

I waited until he broke eye contact first before I turned around and left the room. The guard closed the door behind me, and I quickly scanned the hallway to see if I could deduce anything. Seeing nothing, I walked up the stairs by myself, my escort nowhere to be found. I glanced back at the bar just before I left Bar 53.

The stunning blonde bartender who had taken up way too many of my thoughts in the short time I'd been here?

She was gone.

3

———

HARLOW

"Get the fuck up!"

The shout forced me to freeze in place, not daring to move. The shock wore off, and I glanced to my right. When I saw who the speaker was, I glared at the asshole standing over me. My glare didn't deter him so I hoped my words would.

"We are on our break."

That was true. I was getting some fresh air during one of the few breaks I got during my shifts at Bar 53. It was usually a way to hide from assholes like Ian, but apparently that wouldn't be the case tonight.

Ian Byron was the manager of this establishment. While I didn't know how he treated everyone else, he always had a stick up his ass when it came to me. No matter how much I tried to avoid him, it seemed as if his focus was always on me, no matter the circumstances.

"We're allowed a ten-minute break, Ian."

I couldn't help but look at Emma out of the corner of my eye. Emma tried to keep the peace at all costs, even if it was detrimental to her. We were the exact opposite in that regard because I always felt as if I had nothing left to lose. And if truth be told, I didn't.

"I didn't ask what you were allowed. Get back to work because customers are waiting."

If I could punch him in the face, I would. I had only three months and two weeks left at this gig before I could throw two middle fingers up and waltz on out of here. Even with the clock ticking down, punching Ian in the face would have to be put on the back burner because he was one of Falcone's lackeys.

"Harlow, are you coming?"

I debated whether the consequences would be worth it before I rolled my eyes as I pushed myself off the wall. It was better to get this over with as soon as possible. I pulled out the phone that I'd picked up a couple of weeks ago. My old one had died a horrible death when I forgot it on the hood of my car, never to be seen again. Tracking it proved fruitless, so I assumed it had gotten run over by another vehicle. My replacement was cheaper than my original phone because I hadn't been able to afford anything more. Plus, it wasn't like anyone was going to call me anyway.

Emma leaned over and whispered in my ear, "We have to be careful about rocking the boat here."

"I know, I know." She was right, but that didn't quell the anger I felt.

I was tired of having to deal with this. This treatment had become a day in and day out experience. This job wasn't something that I chose to do. It was something that I was forced into because of my money troubles. If only someone had warned me... I shook my head to clear my thoughts because harping on them wouldn't solve anything. I was in this mess now, and there's nothing I could do to get out of it, except to work for Falcone until I paid my debt off.

Why had I put myself in this situation to begin with? Oh, because I had dreams and ambitions, and I'd worked my ass off to reach my goals yet had fallen flat on my face. Life fucked me over one too many times, and I ended up here at Bar 53 because I owed Falcone a shit ton of money.

But I was working it off, and once I'd washed my hands of him and closed this chapter of my life, I'd get back on track to follow my dreams.

As I wiped down the countertops, I looked up and took in the scene around me.

I watched as more customers filed in. A man, who was the last one to enter with the current rush of patrons, stood near the podium and scanned his surroundings. From where I was standing, I could tell that he was tall with short brown hair that looked as if he'd just run his hands through it. Handsome could easily be used to describe him and that meant he was trouble. Another sign that pointed in that direction? He kept to himself and didn't bother coming over to the bar to order a drink, which was what Bar 53 was known for. I was convinced that he must be here for another reason, and I wasn't willing to assume what it was for.

As I prepared several drinks, I watched as the man spoke to Tim, and I watched Tim freeze before he hurried back to the podium. What was going to happen next?

When our gazes connected, my eyes shot back down and stared at the two glasses in front of me. I didn't understand why I felt so awkward at having been caught staring at the stranger when I would never see him again.

Someone moved out of the corner of my eye and soon I saw Ian was approaching the man. With a slight nod, he turned back around and shot me a glare before leading the man toward a set of stairs that led to the basement. It was where Falcone's office was located, and that was where I assumed all three were going.

This wasn't the first time that I noticed someone I didn't know being led to Falcone's office. But it was the first time that Ian was the one leading someone there.

"I need two shots of tequila."

Emma brought me out of my thoughts. I quickly poured the shots and placed them in front of her. "Need anything else?"

"No." She leaned closer to me and said, "Did you see Ian lead that man downstairs?"

"Yeah. I'm not sure what to think about it, but I know it's not a good thing, however."

"I agree. Watch your back because he has Falcone on his side. Who knows what information he's spilling about any of us."

I shrugged and whispered, "What else can he do to us? He's already ruined our lives."

Emma looked at me before looking down at the two shots in front of her. "I need to serve these up."

I nodded as she picked up the glasses before turning to walk back over to the table. She was right. If Ian went to Falcone about me, it would probably cause him to impose even more interest on the loan that he'd gifted me.

I shouldn't say gifted. It was anything but, and I'd been so desperate at the time that I didn't have a choice. There was no way a bank was going to lend me money to get out of the hole that I dug myself into.

I closed my eyes and took a deep breath. The mask that I liked to wear to hide my emotions was in place. I was excellent at hiding.

I OPENED the door with another deep breath. Shifting Ian to the back of my mind helped, and I focused on closing the bar and heading home. It was a couple of days later, and Ian and I hadn't worked the same shift since my last run-in with him. I mostly avoided him this evening and had done well putting some distance between us. Hopefully not being anywhere near me defused some of the tension between us and he'd get over it.

I was helping with closing and as I glanced around the room, taking the time to study the elegance that Falcone had made sure to instill in the establishment. Outside of my treatment and the reason why I was here, working at Bar 53 wouldn't have been too bad. It was a newer bar that had only been open for a couple of years. Falcone had taken great pride in making sure that Bar 53's appearance and vibe screamed classy and fancy, attracting customers who wanted to come visit one of the latest trendy spots in New York City.

As I walked by myself to the bus stop that would drop me off a couple of blocks away from my apartment, I heard someone call my name. It took half a second for me to recognize the voice and I froze. I turned and found Ian walking out of the shadows toward me.

"What the hell do you want?"

A sly smirk appeared on his face that looked anything but sweet. "Why do you continue to fight me?"

My lip curled in disgust. "Because you're a pain in my ass and will stop at nothing to make my time at Bar 53 a living hell."

He took a step closer to me. "You know it doesn't have to be this way."

This shift in his tone and his closeness to me sounded every alarm in my head. Had he really waited for me to leave work so that he could confront me?

"If you weren't such a bitch, maybe all of this would go away. Or is this you playing hard to get?"

"Of course not, now if you'd excuse me before I punch you in the face..." My words trailed off because he'd grabbed me.

My first reaction was to scream for help, but that option was quickly taken away when his hand flew up to my mouth. My feet dragged on the ground as I bucked my body against him, trying to free myself, to no avail. When he pulled me into an alleyway, my hopes of getting away from him diminished.

Keep fighting, Harlow.

I opened my mouth wider and clamped my teeth down on his hand. This time it was his turn to scream, and I hoped that the sudden pain shooting through his body would give me enough time to break free and run away from him.

I was wrong.

He recovered faster than I thought he would and just as I was about to run away from him, he grabbed me again. This time, his hand landed on my throat as he shoved me up against the wall, pinning me with his body.

My attempts to scream were a failure due to his grip around my neck. A tear fell down my cheek as, once more, my chance of escaping dimmed. He was so much stronger than me.

Keep. Fighting.

His hands haphazardly touched my body, squeezing my breasts before making their way to the hem of my shirt. He roughly pulled it with one hand, and I heard him grunt in approval at what he saw. Him seeing me in this way made me feel even more disgusted. When I tried to cry out again, his grip tightened around my throat, and my hands were left trying to pry his hand off.

If he suffocated me, at least that would remove me from this situation permanently. I could just let go, let it happen because it was inevitable. He was too strong.

No. Don't. Stop. Fighting.

When his hand went toward his belt, the smirk that appeared on his face made a switch go off in my mind. He thought he had me cornered. He thought he'd won.

The hell he had.

My foot connected with his groin hard and caused him to fall to his knees. When air rushed back into my body, I was left gasping.

But I am free.

Without wasting another second, I took off, pulling my bra back into place and my shirt down as I ran. Just as I reached the street, I saw a cab and I flagged him down.

I looked back into the dark alleyway, and I could see Ian was standing up now. His eyes were trained on me. I ran toward the cab and before he could stop completely, I yanked open the cab door and threw myself inside. Just as I slammed the car door shut, Ian had reached the cab, but the driver clicked the locks before he could open the door.

Ian banged on the window of the cab and the driver yelled, "Hey man, fuck off."

That was enough to get Ian to back up and allow the taxi to drive off, taking me away from what could have been an even worse situation.

"Are you okay, miss?"

"Yes, yes I am." I didn't recognize my voice.

"You don't seem okay. Is there anyone I can call for you? I can call the police or take you to the hospital."

Did I look that bad? "I'm fine." I almost told him that there was no one to call but refrained. Yes, he'd saved me from Ian, but who's to know what he might do if he found out that I was going home to an empty apartment?

The driver nodded slightly, and I noticed the volume of the radio increased, filling the silence. It was the first time I'd been content all night and embraced the song about love and happiness, something that I'd only had very few times in my life before it was all snatched away.

4

HARLOW

The morning sun shone through my window the next day like a beacon from a lighthouse. It awakened me from the slumber I'd finally succumbed to only three hours before. I wiped my face, trying to force myself awake, but it didn't do much.

Lack of sleep wouldn't do me any good, but I needed to get up and get moving. I slowly eased my body from the bed, noting every muscle that ached due to being slammed against the wall. As I walked toward my bathroom, I glanced at the dead bolt lock and the chain that further secured my door. Seeing it properly fastened, I continued on, not trusting my legs not to give out at any moment. It didn't take long to reach my bathroom from my bedroom because I lived in a tiny apartment that I could barely afford. It was only because of my landlord's generosity that I was able to live here now.

It wasn't much, but it was home. And more importantly, it was mine. I had little outside of the basics, so it was easy to keep the tiny apartment clean. I'd forced myself on a schedule to keep my space tidy and it had worked. Most of my things were secondhand, and I held on to them for dear life. After all, who knew when I'd be able to afford a replacement?

I stared down at my sink because I couldn't bring myself to look at my reflection in the mirror. Yes, I was in pain, but I'd gotten away from the scumbag. I tried to stop myself from tumbling down the rabbit hole of what might have happened to me if I hadn't escaped, but I couldn't.

He intended to rape me without a doubt, and who knew what else. It wasn't the first time I'd been sexually assaulted, and I knew it contributed to the way I felt about relationships now. I avoided them at all costs because that was what kept me safe.

I looked at my phone, which I must have left in here the night before, and wondered if I should tell Emma about what happened last night.

But what good would that do? Not a damn thing.

I was resigned to the fact that I couldn't tell anyone.

If I told anyone at Bar 53 about what Ian had done to me, I'd be in so much shit. Plus, I didn't want to get anyone else involved nor have them placed on Falcone's hit list. I stared back at my reflection in the mirror, noting the dark circles that had formed under my eyes from a night of not being able to get to sleep.

But I was immediately drawn to the mark on my throat. The imprint of his hand around my neck was more pronounced today than it had been last night.

"Shit," I mumbled to myself as I touched the bruised skin. Luckily, it didn't hurt. I also noticed the scratch on my shoulder looked more gnarly this morning and was more sore today than it had been last night. The adrenaline had worn off. Makeup would be required before I headed into the bar, or I knew someone would start asking questions I couldn't answer.

I tossed my blonde hair into a bun on the top of my head and pulled at my face, examining every pore that I could see. The slight blue tinge under my eyes became even more apparent with my hair up. Or maybe it was just me being overly critical.

I felt as if I looked older than my twenty-three years, but there was nothing I could do about that. Instead, I let my head fall as I leaned over the sink. My breath was shaky as I tried and failed to catch it.

With another deep breath, I stood up tall and pushed my shoulders back, hoping to grant myself a boost of confidence that I didn't feel. I turned the faucet on and watched as water fell from the spout. My hands landed underneath it and I drew the water to my face. I enjoyed the cooling sensation that it left and watched several droplets fall from my body before I reached over and grabbed the towel that I'd used the night before. I'd come home and immediately scrubbed my body, hoping to remove the feel of Ian's touch on my skin, but it hadn't worked. The only reason I hadn't had a nightmare the night before was because I barely slept.

I grabbed my phone, left the bathroom, and walked back over to my bed to make it. When I finished, my eyes landed on a picture that I kept on my kitchen counter. I picked it up and stared at it, memorizing every element, and committing the moment to memory once again.

The photo was taken about a year ago at a bookshop near New York University, my alma mater. I was in my last semester of college and Mama Robinson had taken me out for coffee as a treat. Spending money on expensive books and coffee was a rare occurrence due to the lack of money we both had, so I'd treasured the moment and the fun we had together. I treasured it even more now that she was gone.

You're going to own one of these one day.

Her words coursed through my mind just before a drop of water landed on the frame. The idea that I would own a bookshop one day was so far beyond the realm of possibility, especially given the money I owed Falcone.

Usually looking at the photo gave me warm and fuzzy feelings. The last time I'd felt this way was when Mama Robinson had taken me in and given me a home that I could call my own. She raised me when no one else would.

I barely kept it together when I thought about Mama Robinson and how my life had changed when she died. She was the only one who gave two shits about me. The years we'd spent together were beautiful and cut way too short when she died unexpectedly from a heart attack.

There I was, mourning the loss of someone near and dear to me and wondering how I was going to pay for her funeral costs. Like me, Mama Robinson was alone in this world, with no family, and together we'd become one. Sometimes I dreamed about Mama Robinson and wondered what she would think of me right now.

I shouldn't have borrowed the money from Falcone to pay for her funeral, but there was no way that I wasn't going to make sure that she rested in peace, and all of her affairs were in order. She'd given me so much when no one else would have, and it was the least that I could do, even if I wished she'd been better prepared for death than she had been.

I sat down on my freshly made bed and debated what I

should do with myself. Hibernating in my apartment until I was forced to go out seemed like a good plan, especially since I didn't have to work today. I had enough food that I would have meals for several days, so I didn't have to worry about that either.

My eyes danced around the small room and landed on the bookshelf in the far corner. I had plenty of books that I needed to catch up on and read. It was small, but held most of my books, so for that, I was grateful. Many of them were bought secondhand or I'd gotten them for free. Going to the library was great, but there was something about being able to own some of your favorites and read them whenever you wanted.

With my decision made, I walked over to the bookshelf and pulled out an old favorite of mine. I returned to my bed and wrapped my comforter around me. I began to read, transporting myself to another place and time where everything was much better than here.

5

HARLOW

Ian sneered at me as he walked past me on the way toward the kitchen. The busted lip and the cut that was on his neck after I fought him off looked even better to me this morning than what I'd seen just before I took off down the street. Although I'd beaten myself up due to me spending money I barely had on a cab, it got me away from the asshole as quickly as possible and potentially saved my life. I'd survived.

While his behavior was a nuisance, he hadn't attempted to talk to me since I'd fled in the cab. I assumed part of that was due to whenever he was around, I tried to make sure that I was with someone else to avoid us being alone together.

When he walked past the bar for the hundredth time, he slid a note in my direction. I debated if I should toss the damn thing in the garbage or open it. The latter won out.

You're going to pay for what you did.

I licked my lips nervously before I put the note in my pocket. This might be worth keeping around in case he did do something, and I needed proof. Then again, who was I going to tell? Falcone probably had them paid off and knowing him, he'd probably do anything to make sure that Ian didn't get on their radar. After all, it might lead to some suspicion being thrown on his business dealings.

That brought back memories of the man I'd seen heading down toward Falcone's office a few days ago. I knew he had to be dirty if he was having a meeting with Falcone while Bar 53 was open, but that didn't mean that I didn't mind looking at him while he'd been waiting for Ian.

Everything about him screamed tall, dark, and mysterious with a dangerous tilt. And I'd watched him staring at me, as if he was peeling each layer of me back until he reached my soul. Just the thought of him sent a chill through my body.

I was quickly pulled out of my thoughts of the stranger when Ian entered my line of sight again. The glare that he gave me told me this wouldn't be the end, even though he turned on his heel and stormed out of the room. I blew out the breath I'd been holding and rolled my shoulders back. While I won the battle several days ago, I knew the war was far from over.

Why did he have to be here today? I'd hoped he wouldn't be around because he wasn't on the schedule, but I found out a few hours ago that he was going to be on the same shift as me. I glanced at the clock on the wall just as I grabbed a rag to wipe down the bar. I had two hours to deal with the rest of this bullshit. Only a few more months and my debt will be paid in full.

When Ian didn't reappear, I took a deep breath and brushed thoughts of him aside. I had a job to do, and I was determined to do it. It didn't take much for me to get back into the rhythm of serving drinks after my dustup with Ian.

Emma wasn't working today, so I didn't have to worry about her.

Emma wasn't cut out for life like this and as a result, she and I had grown closer as the months had passed. Although she was a couple of years older than me, I'd taken on more of a big sister role in our friendship because she didn't like confrontation and there was no way I was going to let anyone walk all over me or anyone else I cared about.

"Harlow."

My name on his lips made me stop mid movement. I glanced at Ian before I finished making a patron's drink.

I will not cause a scene. I will not cause a scene.

"Yes?" I handed the customer their drink.

"Falcone wants to see you."

For some reason, I wasn't surprised to hear that. Given how much Ian had been hovering around me, I suspected that something like this was going to happen. The smile on Ian's face proved to me that this was all his doing.

Without checking to see if I was following him, Ian walked out from behind the bar, and I quickly wiped my hands on one of the towels I kept in my back pocket.

I made eye contact with one of the other bartenders and pointed to the customer, letting him know that he needed to ring this woman up. I walked down the stairs as quickly as I could, and Falcone's guard gestured for me to enter the office before closing the door behind me. I wasn't shocked to find Ian already in there, standing just to the left of Falcone, who was seated at his desk.

"Harlow, I heard you're giving Ian trouble."

It took everything in me to not roll my eyes and to bite back the cuss that threatened to fall from my lips. Of course the asshole went and blabbed to Falcone and more than likely left out how he'd antagonized me since I started here.

I chose my words carefully. "I've been a loyal employee who has been working to pay off the loan you gave me. I'm always on time and haven't missed a day I was scheduled to work."

Falcone nodded once. "This is all true unless you're keeping something from me, Ian."

"No, Sir," Ian replied.

I cupped one hand over my other, letting both rest in front of me. I gently squeezed one of my pressure points to try to remain as calm as possible. "Ian and I have never seen eye to eye, but I've never let it impede my performance here."

"That's not necessarily true, Sir."

My remaining calm flew out the window. "You mean when you tried to rape me?"

"You fucking liar," Ian said as he turned his body toward me like he was about to attack me.

My fight-or-flight instinct kicked in. Before either one of us could act, Falcone held his hand up.

"Did you try to rape her, Ian?"

I watched as his eyes darted between me and Falcone. "No, she's been playing hard to get ever since she got here and I—"

My mouth opened wide as Ian tried to accuse me of wanting him to attack me. "You've got to be fucking kidding me, you piece of—"

"Enough!"

Falcone's words stopped both Ian and me. Falcone stared at Ian for a moment before looking at me and I watched as a light bulb went off in his head.

"Change of plan, Harlow. You're not going to work at Bar 53 any longer."

I folded my arms across my chest. "You're going to let me go?"

His smirk made my heart sink. "Oh, no, no, no. I've decided that I want my payment in full sooner rather than later."

My stomach bottomed out. There was no way I was going to have anywhere close to how much I owed him right now.

"But we had an agreement."

"Yes, that I set the stipulations for and that I can change them at will. It's all in the contract you signed, remember?"

Falcone looked at me and a shiver ran down my spine. I couldn't quite describe it, but he wasn't looking at me as if I were a person anymore. He reached over and grabbed his office phone before pressing one button.

"Rose? I have another one for you for the party."

He waited a couple of seconds before hanging up the phone. His stare had never strayed from me, but this time he spoke.

"We require your services elsewhere. I'll send a car to pick you up on Saturday."

I was afraid of the answer, but I asked the question anyway. "And if I don't go?"

The look in his eyes almost made me take a step back. When he looked down at his desk, I took the opportunity to breathe before the air left my lungs in a rush. He'd picked up a gun that I hadn't seen on his desk and the next thing I knew, I was staring down the end of a gun barrel.

"I'll kill you."

6

ACE

I opened the file again and scanned the page for the millionth time. The words hadn't changed, nor had I expected them to.

The red envelope with gold trim that I placed next to it just moments before had taken up most of my attention. I knew where the invitation had come from, but it didn't do much to settle the feeling in my stomach. Then again, that could have been due to the room I was in.

Sitting behind this desk felt foreign to me even though I'd lived here for a few years now. I'd recently started using it to conduct business, but it still didn't feel right. I'd heard how often my grandfather held meetings here, and it felt as if I was imposing. That was one of the reasons why I didn't invite too many people here or host anyone. I hadn't changed much since he left because I'd had plenty of other things to worry about.

My grandfather loved dark woods and featured them a lot throughout his home. It made things seem dreary throughout most of the rooms. It fit my mood most of the time, so maybe that was another thing we had in common outside of me looking like him when he was my age. If anyone doubted it, the portrait that he'd placed of himself above the fireplace in this office would prove them to be a liar.

I reached over and grabbed the coffee that I shouldn't be having this late in the day and took a sip. It was one of the habits I kept after I quit smoking.

As if I'd manifested its existence, I opened the top drawer and saw the pack of cigarettes that I'd forgotten I kept in there. I should have thrown them away, but couldn't bring myself to do so. Would it be worth it to take a hit? I'd quit a while ago, but the urge to smoke right now was there. Sitting in the drawer next to it was an older photo that had seen better days. It was easy to see that it was a photo of my mother and grandfather during happier times. Based on the year written on the back of the photo and their friendly nature with one another, it was clear it was before I was born. One would have never thought he would throw his only child out on the streets just a few short years later.

Burying those thoughts as quickly as they appeared, I put the photo back in the desk drawer where it belonged and closed it decisively.

For some reason, Parker Townsend entered my mind. I still hadn't heard from him after our brief encounter after the Chevaliers meeting. I'd expected to hear from him sooner and it wasn't as if he didn't have my contact information. Even though I'd had more pressing matters to deal with, him wanting to meet with me sat in the back of my mind more often than I cared to admit. What could he possibly want?

But what weighed on me more was the envelope sitting

on my desk. I picked up the red envelope and tapped it on my desk. I flipped it over and ran my finger along the crease that held the flap closed. I'd recognized it immediately as Falcone's and knew it was an invitation to the special party he was hosting. The envelope reminded me of the décor in his office, a mixture of deep reds and golds made it stand out among the regular mail.

Instead of continuing to prolong the inevitable, I shifted some papers and found what I had in mind. A letter opener that had been in here longer than I'd lived here, or hell maybe longer than I'd been alive. Touching it made me think of my grandfather and the unnecessary trauma he caused, but I pushed it to the side and opened the envelope. Inside lay a gold-colored piece of cardstock with typed lettering on it.

"'You've been invited to attend a party hosted by Clay Falcone,'" I read out loud.

I scanned the rest of the invitation. I knew that the party would be anything but a joyous occasion, but I focused on the mission that I was given. Find out as much information as I could about Falcone's operations out of this particular property. If I found out who was leaking information about the Vitale crime family, that would be a bonus. We knew that there was more going on than just parties being thrown there, but what? Drugs? Weapons? All the above?

"Sir?"

I looked up from the invitation and found Anderson standing in the doorway. Going from being the scum of the earth to having everything I have now was a complete mind-fuck and something that I still wasn't used to. That included having a home with a butler who referred to me as "sir". No matter how many times I corrected him to call me Ace, he reverted to "sir," so I'd given up.

He'd called my grandfather "sir" since he'd started working for him twenty years ago, so I assumed the greeting had just stuck. "Would you like anything before I retire?"

I thought for a moment before shaking my head. "No, I have everything I need. Thank you."

"You're welcome, Sir." And he left just as quietly as he came.

I stood up from the big brown desk that took up a significant portion of what had now become my office. But none of this felt as if it were mine because in reality, it wasn't. When the chair creaked under my weight, I made a note to myself to tell Anderson to order me a new chair.

I'd inherited all of this from a man I barely knew. And I resented him because of it. He'd had the power to change my life in ways that many could only imagine, but he'd chosen not to. Instead, he waited until he knew he needed to make sure an heir was in place to enact such a change. And while I stood in the home that he built, my feelings toward him grew colder every time I thought about him. There was no way that I could change the past, but even though my grandfather was thousands of miles away, it still felt as if sometimes he was still trying to make my life a living hell.

Coming from someone who now lived in an estate that spanned many acres, it seemed foolish to think in such a way, but my life hadn't always been this way and Jerald Bolton was one reason why.

My eyes drifted back to the invitation that now glittered under the light shining from my desk lamp, tempting me in a way. Any thoughts I had about my childhood and my family were shifted to the side and I was determined. This was an easy assignment that would be wrapped up quickly. After all, this was nothing more than a pissing contest over power between Will and Falcone. I leaned forward, picked up my office phone, and dialed the number on the invitation. It rang several times before a woman answered on the other end.

"Hello?"

I spoke without hesitation. "This is Ace Bolton, and I'd like to RSVP for the party at Clay Falcone's place this Saturday."

7

———

HARLOW

What the fuck had I gotten myself into?

Technically, this was forced upon me so I could cut myself some slack. I could murder Ian with my bare hands, but who knew where that would leave me. Maybe it wouldn't be in this car on the way to who knows where. Maybe I wouldn't be left wondering what lay on the road ahead, literally, and figuratively.

I'd done my best to prepare for whatever situation might arise. I wore my Bar 53 uniform since Falcone mentioned that my services would be required. The black button-down and black slacks matched the dreariness I felt about this situation. I'd thrown my hair up into a sleek ponytail to keep it out of my face for what I assumed would be a long night. If I was going to be paying off the rest of my debt tonight, I assumed Falcone was going to make sure he worked me to the bone.

My fingers drummed along to another song on the radio, although I couldn't tell you what it was. I could hear it playing, but for some reason, I couldn't place it no matter how hard I tried to focus. My attention was trained on what might be waiting for me when this car stopped.

I wasn't keeping track of how long we'd been driving for, but I noticed when we left the city limits. Long gone were the city's skyscrapers and in its place was more land and space than one could ever dream of. If I wasn't uncomfortable about the situation before, I would have been more so now.

Would this count as kidnapping? Yes, I'd willingly gotten into the vehicle, but all of this was happening because I didn't have a choice.

Not having any other options further tightened the knot in my stomach. I looked into the rearview mirror and found the driver of the vehicle staring back at me for a moment before his eyes drifted back toward the road.

I noticed that he had been stealing quick glances at me every so often, but he never said a word. I'd finally had enough.

"Where are we going?" I asked.

But silence was my only answer. Something told me he probably wouldn't respond, so I shouldn't have been shocked when he didn't. Maybe I'd put all my hope into him being somewhat of a saving grace for me during this time of emotional turmoil. It was foolish to have even a smidge of optimism given who was involved. This was more than likely my worst nightmare.

I watched as trees flew past my window, and when the driver shifted the vehicle to leave the highway, my anxiety increased. I cupped my hands together and squeezed, forcing my hands to hold one another as I tried to hold myself together before I reached the end of this journey.

The drive continued for several more miles before we

turned down a quiet street. When the car pulled up to a closed gate, my fingers froze. Nothing on the gate gave away where we were, but when the gates opened and we drove down the road, I was able to answer one of my questions.

The mansion that lay before us was majestic in nature but I hadn't expect anything different from Falcone. We slowly drove up the driveway, giving me the opportunity to look around. I glanced down at my hands and let them relax after I saw the imprint my nails had left on my skin. We pulled to a stop in front of the home, and the door quickly opened and out rushed a woman who looked to be in her early fifties. Instead of my silent driver opening the car door, she opened it and gestured for me to exit the vehicle.

"Come on! We need to head inside because we don't have any time to waste," she said.

My heart lurched into my throat as I wondered what could possibly be this dire that we had to rush and do it. I stumbled out of the car, trying to move as fast as my legs would take me, but my nerves seemed to have the last laugh. On the plus side, at least she seemed willing to talk, unlike the driver I had just spent who knows how much time with.

Once I was out of the car, she looked at me and shook her head. "First things first. Give me your phone."

"Excuse me?" I'd finally found something to say.

"We don't have any time to waste," she repeated. "Hand over your phone. You won't be needing it for the time being anyway."

"I'm not handing over my phone."

"Look, I'm just doing what I've been told to do. You can take it up with Mr. Falcone or hand me the phone."

I debated arguing with her, but I was going to do everything I could do to avoid being near Falcone. She'd made a good point. Outside of being able to call the police if something happened, what did I need my phone for? And would anyone believe me if I did call the authorities? Plus, it wasn't as if someone was going to check up on me.

Emma might shoot me a text message, but I wasn't on the schedule to work today, and I'd just seen her yesterday as I was secretly finishing up my last few days at Bar 53.

Her stare and her hand on her hip told me that her patience was growing thin.

Before I handed it over to her, I looked down at the device and noticed that my reception was slowly going from full service to no bars. Yes, I sometimes had problems getting service while I was inside of a building, but I chalked it up to owning a shitty cell phone. But never had I had issues with having service while outside. How remote was this place?

I handed the phone to her, and she placed it in her pocket without a second thought. "Follow me."

With that, she turned on her heel and walked away from me and back toward the house. I found myself staring behind her before hearing the car that brought me here pull away, effectively leaving me stranded. Since I had no other choice outside of trying to hike to someone else's home or back to the highway, I followed the woman up the stairs and into the enormous house in front of me.

To keep up with the woman's clipped pace, I ignored most of my surroundings. Once we were in the foyer, she kept walking toward the stairs, and I almost stopped her to ask her why we were heading this way. I should have been headed toward the bar area or kitchen.

"Excuse me, but where are we going?"

"This way," she said.

So much for answering my question.

Every so often, she would look over her shoulder, I assumed to check to see if I was keeping up with her. She led me down a long hallway and stopped in front of the last door on the left. Before she could open it, I heard a thump coming from a door on my right and she just shook her head.

"Ignore that," she said as she twisted the knob and opened the door before ushering me inside. She joined me inside and slammed the door behind her, making me jump.

Before I could do anything else, she grasped my cheeks in her hands.

"You look pretty rough, dear," the woman said as she examined my face much like I'd done several days before.

I wasn't offended by her comment because it was true. This had been a hellish week, and something deep down told me that it was only just getting started.

Her tone was much different than when she'd first retrieved me from the car.

"It's been a rough few days, if I have to be honest."

"And tonight won't be much better. You're the last one to arrive, so we need to work fast."

"Does this have to do with the event tonight?"

She nodded and walked over to another door that I soon confirmed was a closet.

"By the way, what's your name?"

She peeked out of the closet before responding. "Silly me, I should have introduced myself, but I was in such a hurry. I'm Rose and you're Harlow, correct?"

"Yes, that's right."

Rose swiped through several garments while glancing at me.

"You're about a size six and about five-six, correct?"

How did she know that? It was obvious that she knew more about me than I knew about her. "Uh, yes, that's right."

"Okay. Why don't you take a shower while I pull out a few pieces that might work for tonight?"

"I showered before I got here," I said as I watched her remove a dress from the closet. "Why do I need to wear a dress tonight? Our usual uniform is this."

Rose paused her movements before looking at me over her shoulder. "You don't know why you're here, do you?"

I crossed my arms over my chest, suddenly feeling exposed and wondering how much I was in the dark about what was going on. "I'm here to bartend at an event tonight."

"Oh, no, dear." She shook her head. I could see pity rising in her eyes. "You're here to be auctioned off to the highest bidder."

8

———————

HARLOW

Had she just said what I thought she said? "No, I'm not. I want to go home now. I'll find another way to pay Falcone back."

"I'm sorry, but this is the only choice you have, dear."

I walked up to the woman and put my hand on her arm. I debated my options and chose something I'd never thought I'd do: beg. "Please, you can just sneak me out the back door or something and no one would have to know."

"I wish I could, but it would be a matter of life or death for both of us if I did." She swallowed hard and then said, "There's one thing you should do, however."

"What's that?"

"Pray that the person who bids on you isn't a complete monster."

I choked back tears at her words. Someone who was willing to bid on another person under these circumstances had to be a savage. I couldn't wrap my mind around it as Rose pushed me toward another door.

"So, like I said, please shower quickly so we can get you ready."

"There has to be some other way."

This time she looked me in the eye and said, "You and I both know there isn't or else you wouldn't be here right now, Harlow. The more you stall, the later you'll be, and neither one of us wants that."

I saw a glimpse of fear pass across her face before she pushed me toward another door in the room. When I opened the door, I wasn't surprised to find a bathroom that was probably large enough to fit my tiny apartment in. It was almost like walking into a fancy hotel bathroom that I'd seen on television growing up. The number of beauty products that lined a portion of one of the walls astounded me, but also made me feel sick to my stomach. How many women had come before me and had done this exact thing against their will?

To make it through tonight, I turned my attention to the shower and flipped it on. Without a moment's hesitation, the water flowed from the sprinkler head, and I had to admit it was one of the most breathtaking things I'd ever seen.

Growing up, sometimes being able to find a working bath or shower had been difficult, and even now that I had my own apartment, I swore that my shower was barely holding on. Having a showerhead that worked efficiently and had warm water flowing from it almost immediately would have been a life-changing experience for me if I wasn't so desperate to get out of this fucked-up auction.

When I stepped into the shower, I basked in the short-term glory. Feeling luxurious for five minutes loosened my nerves, but once I stepped out of the shower with a towel firmly wrapped around my body, my anxiety rose. I was one step closer to meeting the fate that would be laid out for me tonight.

"Everything all right, dear?"

"Uh, yes. I'll be out in a moment."

I used a vanilla-scented lotion that I found and wrapped a bathrobe around my naked body before walking back out into the bedroom. I noticed Rose had laid out several dresses on the bed, I'm assuming one for me to choose tonight. When she turned to me, she gave me a small smile, one I returned, having decided that there was nothing I could do to change what was going to unfold.

"Why don't you try on these dresses quickly and then we'll decide which one is best?"

I nodded and asked, "Do I get something to put on underneath?"

"I knew I was forgetting something." Rose walked over to the dresser and pulled out what I could only describe as black lingerie. I swallowed hard again as she handed them to me.

"I'll turn around while you put those on and then we can get started."

When she turned her back to me, I disrobed and put the underwear on. "I'm ready."

She turned back around and looked at me before clapping her hands once. "You look way better than when you came in here. More alive is how I would describe it. But your neck..."

That was ironic because I felt more dead if I had to be honest. I grasped the part of my body that was now the source of concern. I'd temporarily forgotten that I hadn't put makeup to cover the bruises on my neck and the scar on my shoulder.

"It's not something I want to talk about."

Rose nodded. "Fine, we'll cover it up once we've figured out a dress."

She handed me a black dress first and I slipped it onto my body. I walked over to a full-length mirror and took in my appearance.

She shook her head. "This doesn't work."

"I agree."

"Okay, let's try another."

We went through all the dresses on the bed and still hadn't picked one.

"There was one I was debating but hadn't pulled out. I see a fire in your eyes. You will make it through this. In fact, I think this dress here would be perfect for you."

She walked over to the closet and pulled out a garment bag. She unzipped it before handing me a red dress.

I curled my hair into loose curls with the curling wand that Rose found and worked on my makeup that thankfully had been provided. Even the bruises on my neck and the scratch on my shoulder looked hardly noticeable. When I looked back into the mirror, I didn't recognize the woman standing before me.

"Are you ready? I believe you're up first."

"Y-yes I am."

It was showtime.

My heart was thundering in my chest. In fact, I wondered if it would make a run for it to escape the prison my body had created for it. It felt as if I was in a prison as I waited for my turn to be called to the stage.

The feeling of wanting to throw up was present and I wondered if it would be worth making a run to the bathroom. Hell, maybe if I ran into the bathroom, that might buy me some time to escape.

I turned to Rose and said, "May I use this restroom?"

I gave her a small smile in hopes that she would trust me enough to allow me to do so. My haphazard plan might fall apart, but I had to try something.

She smiled back at me and leaned over to talk to the man who'd directed us where to wait backstage. He looked at her just before he looked at me. "Sure, but make it quick."

My heart skipped a beat when the woman turned to me and led me to one of the bathrooms on this floor. Without another word, I walked inside and immediately took in my surroundings.

The bathroom was decorated in the same manner as the house and to my surprise, included a wall that was partially covered by a curtain. Could that be my way out?

I locked the bathroom door, hoping to slow down anyone that might try to walk in or question why I was taking so long. I walked across the floor and pulled the curtain back.

I could have cried tears of joy when I found that there was a window behind the curtain. I pushed on it at first and it didn't budge. In my haste, I hadn't noticed that the window was locked, so I quickly turned the knobs and pushed again. This time it moved, and I opened the window several inches and peered outside.

If I climbed out of the window, it wouldn't be that far of a fall, so maybe I wouldn't get hurt. But was that a risk I was willing to take? Yes, the hell I would if it meant that I would be free from the highest bidder. I looked around to see if I could find anything that would help give me a small boost so that I could climb out of the window. I found a small ledge that I might be able to balance on if I acted quickly.

Without giving it much of a second thought, I placed my foot on the ledge and just as I was about to toss my leg out of the window, I saw something that turned my blood cold. Guards with high-powered guns were walking near the house, I assume ready to attack anyone who crossed them.

A small tear slid down my cheek, potentially ruining the makeup that painted my face as I realized once again how bleak this situation was. I might be able to outrun someone, even in this dress, but there was no way I would be able to outrun someone who was a trained marksman, ready to shoot and kill.

Although I owed Falcone money, there was no doubt in my mind that he would have no issue with one of his men killing me. Yes, I was worthless dead, but he'd probably get great pleasure in seeing my dead body after he'd sent me here to take part in this auction.

A knock on the door made me jump. "Harlow, it's time."

"Give me a minute."

When she didn't say anything else, I glanced back at the window and literally felt my window of opportunity closing on me. With a heavy heart, I flushed the toilet before heading over to the sink to wash my hands. Once I'd dried them off, I looked at myself in the mirror.

My makeup was still holding up well, which was a relief. No matter what life threw at me, I promised myself I wouldn't be rattled. Today was one of those days where it was hard to do so.

I walked out of the bathroom and joined Rose with a tight

smile. She rushed me back to where we'd been waiting before and soon, I felt myself following the auctioneer.

Before where I felt as if I was being swept into a tornado as I traveled through the house, now it felt as if time had stopped. I studied the scene that unfolded in front of me as I stepped onto the makeshift stage that had been set up in this great room. The décor in the room was elaborately designed in red, gold, and black, very different from the vibe Falcone had chosen through his décor choices at Bar 53. Maybe he intentionally designed this space to look like hell to further torment the people that had to stand on this stage.

When all eyes were on me, I stood up straight and cupped one hand with the other and squeezed, willing my heart to stop racing. I started repeating a mantra to myself that I hoped would eventually force me to believe it.

You will get through this. You will get through this.

This was really happening. I was being auctioned off to the highest bidder. The auctioneer didn't even turn to look at me before he cleared his throat and started speaking. The small amount of compassion that I'd gotten from Rose wasn't anywhere to be found. It felt as if I'd been thrown to the wolves.

The auctioneer didn't bother saying my name when introducing me and gave only my body measurements and a brief rundown of my "skills" that no one else should know unless I told them. The feeling of violation coursed through me as I felt like an intangible thing instead of a person. The thought of that had been in the back of my mind for some time, but not even being referred to by my name was more painful than I'd imagined.

I fought with myself as I tried not to sink back into old

habits and thoughts that haunted me throughout my child-hood. I needed to stay strong or else I would crumble right in front of all of these vultures who would have no problem eating me alive.

And then I saw him.

When our eyes connected, I could have cried. The vulner-ability I felt increased tenfold as I tried to keep it together. Although I didn't know him, just seeing his familiar face made me feel a million different things at once.

Due to the bright lights and where he was sitting, I couldn't tell what color his eyes were, but I felt drawn to him for some reason. I tried to break the stare between us, but I couldn't. A strong urge in my body made me feel called to him in hopes that he would save me from this hell.

9

———

ACE

I nodded at the person who opened the front door for me as I stepped inside the home. Although I made it a point to be a few minutes early, it seemed as if a few people milling about also had the same idea.

Fucking sleazeballs everywhere.

That was the perfect word to describe the people in this home. I hated these types of people, the arrogant assholes who didn't give a damn about anyone else, but I could deal with them for the time being because I had only one thing on my mind: gathering as much intel as I could to take back to Will.

What was Falcone up to out here? What was clear was that he knew how to throw a party fit for his guests.

I walked past two men who were sitting in two chairs next to one another. Both sized me up as I walked past, and one even had the audacity to suck on his cigar and attempt to send a billow of smoke my way. My inclination was to have a little chat with him, but I refused to let the asshole shift my focus. There would be a time and place to deal with him later.

"Mr. Bolton."

I turned to face the person who had called my name. I didn't use an alternate identity when I went to meet with Falcone because it would have been too easy to identify who I was.

I raised an eyebrow at the woman standing in front of me. It was interesting that she knew who I was because I hadn't submitted a picture to go along with my RSVP. So, who here was keeping tabs on me? I could hazard a guess who she worked for.

"Follow me and I'll show you to your seat."

I spared one last glance at the two men before following the woman through a set of doors that opened into a larger sitting area. The living space was organized with a makeshift stage near a set of windows with the blinds drawn. Chairs were lined up on the opposite side, ready for everyone to view the stage. People were mingling with one another and as we walked by, the woman whose name I never caught gently told them that the show would be starting soon.

"Here's your seat, Mr. Bolton. I hope you enjoy your time here tonight."

I looked at her for a moment before I took my seat. *What the hell has Kingston gotten me into?*

A survey of the room didn't give me much insight into what was going on. People were chit-chatting with one another, and I seemed to be the only one who didn't have anyone to talk to. Which was how I preferred it.

Everyone around me started making their way to their

seats, and I looked down at my phone. I found Kingston's phone number and sent him a text message.

Me: *What the hell is this all about?*

As I was typing the message, I noticed my phone's signal starting to waver. I'd noticed that my signal had weakened as I was pulling up to the house, but once inside, my phone's signal was strong. Now I was slowly watching it diminish again until my phone displayed no bars. There was no way that Kingston was going to be able to reach me now. Who was messing with the reception here? Before I could ponder it further, the murmurs lowered, and I wondered why. When I looked up, I found a man in a suit who looked as if he'd thrown it on in a hurry. Next to him stood a woman who immediately took my breath away.

That was until I saw her face. The blonde bartender from Falcone's bar. When our eyes met, I saw fear shining in hers.

The man next to her cleared his throat and said, "Who's ready to bid on this lovely woman in red?"

With all eyes on her, the woman in red continued to look at me, almost calling out to me with her eyes, begging me to bid on her.

I could hear the host talking about her, but my attention was trained on her. When she finally broke our stare, I watched as she looked down at her dress before tossing her shoulders back and straightening her posture. She became more stunning to me at that very moment. My hand grasped the paddle.

"That would be a nice piece of ass, wouldn't it?"

I shifted my attention to the man sitting next to me. He was an older man and had been quietly talking to the man next to him when I sat down. But clearly, that was over.

"One hundred thousand dollars, to the gentleman in the hat. Can I get two hundred thousand?"

I could hear the man next to me snickering, thinking that he had won his prize. Too bad he didn't know how wrong he was. I lifted my paddle high enough for the auctioneer to see it, and when he pointed at me, I nodded. I glanced at the man next to me and saw him glare at me out of the corner of his eye.

"We now have two hundred thousand. Can we get three hundred thousand?"

The fucker's hand immediately shot in the air, and he said, "Five hundred thousand dollars."

The auctioneer's and the blonde bartender's mouths dropped open. This man either really wanted to have her or he was doing it to stick it to me because he was pissed he had competition.

The auctioneer recovered first. "Okay, we have five hundred thousand dollars. Going once, going twice..."

I lifted my paddle calmly before I announced, "One million dollars."

Gasps could be heard all around the room as everyone's eyes turned to me. Instead of focusing on the attention that had been drawn to me, I turned to the man next to me, daring him to bet any higher. He swallowed hard, but refused to look to his right. I knew that he could feel the heat of my gaze on him.

"We have one million dollars. Going once... going twice.... Sold to the man in the navy blue suit. Please come up and claim your prize."

As I made my way up to the stage, a man walked up to the woman in red and gestured for her to walk off the stage. I could see the inner debate she was having with herself. Instead, she obeyed and followed the man who had called to her. What felt like an electric current passed through my body as I watched her walk in front of me, taking the opportunity to watch the way the dress was molded to her body, as if it were made just for her. A thought flashed through my mind that involved ripping the fabric off her body. Inch. By. Inch.

We were led to a room that contained a long table and a few chairs but wasn't decorated nearly as elaborately as the other rooms I'd walked through in the home.

"Who are you?" I asked.

Both the woman and man looked at me over their shoulders, but my eyes were trained on her. I noticed as the woman began to talk, he spoke over her.

"Name is Tomas."

I glared at him for talking when he wasn't being spoken to, and he hurried forward to put distance between us. He stopped at a closed door that wasn't too far off from where we were all gathered just moments before. Tomas opened the door and we filed in.

I watched as the smarmy-looking man in front of me took a seat first and the woman in red sat down on the other side of the table, as far away as she could get from him. Her eyes jumped between the two of us before I took a seat next to her and leveled my gaze at the man in front of us.

"This is a contract that dictates you'll pay the one million to Falcone in exchange for her. Whatever you choose to do with her is up to your discretion."

When he referred to the woman in red, I caught a glimpse of her out of the corner of my eye and saw that while her hands were resting in her lap, she wasn't the picture of calm. She was squeezing her hand for dear life, and I couldn't help but wonder if she would erupt.

Not that any of it would matter. It wouldn't change anything about our deal. I read over the contract before signing. I pulled out my phone to organize the transfer of money. As I placed my phone down on the table, there was a knock on the door and the woman who escorted me to my seat entered.

"Tomas, if you're done wrapping this up, you're needed to do the contract work for another transaction in the room next door." She quickly closed the door behind her after her announcement.

My eyes drifted over to the blonde bartender because I couldn't help but be drawn to her and to her reaction about what was happening around her. It was easy to see that she wasn't pleased. She was still tightly gripping her hand as if that was the only thing keeping her sane.

I reread the papers in front of me, taking my time even though Tomas had to leave. Hearing him tap his foot underneath the table, but not being able to say anything to me because I was signing over a large sum of money to his boss, was enjoyable.

Another knock on the door made the beautiful woman next to me jump and we all looked up. It was Falcone himself.

His stare landed on Tomas, and he said, "You may leave."

He scrambled to get up and make way for his boss before closing the door behind him.

"When I invited you here, I didn't expect you to make a purchase right away, Mr. Bolton. I thank you."

I shrugged and pushed the contract toward him. "When I want something, I get it."

"I like that attitude... and I think you're going to get plenty with her." Before I could say anything else, he said, "Do you have any other business to attend to here or will you be leaving?"

I thought about the original reason I'd come here and said, "I do want to see what else might come up for sale."

I thought I heard her growl beside me, but I couldn't be sure. If what I said kept things calm and cool between me and Falcone, then that was the goal. If he found out the real reason I was here, then I knew there would be blood spilled.

"Understandable. She'll be upstairs until you're ready to claim her."

The blonde bartender clenched her fists. Her reaction was unsurprising, and it was the first time I'd seen emotion out of her since she walked out to face the figurative guillotine.

"I'll have someone fetch her." He turned away from both of us and the woman in red's hands were also turning red given how hard she was squeezing them. I placed a hand on her knee without thinking and she jerked her leg away from me.

"She's very feisty, be warned."

"I can handle her." This time I looked her in the eye, showing both him and her that I was in charge of this situation. Out of the corner of my eye, I noticed that I had gotten two very different responses. The smile on Falcone's face was very appreciative and in agreement with my words. She looked as if she would kill me if given the chance. And I didn't blame her one bit.

10

———————

ACE

I took my time looking around the room as I watched the auction continue. Everyone's eyes were trained on the stage, wondering who the next contestant was going to be. Sitting here watching this all occur would have made anyone feel sick to their stomachs. But me? The only thing that mattered was saving her, a woman whose name I didn't even know. In some ways, some might view it as foolish and reckless, but I didn't give a shit what other people thought. My only focus was on getting her out of here and telling Kingston and Will about this party.

I glanced at my phone and found that my signal returned, and I quickly sent a text to my butler, but there was still nothing from Kingston.

"Congrats on getting that beauty in red."

I turned and found the fucker I'd outbid for the blonde bartender. His tone was sarcastic, and his expression matched it. He looked a little too smug and I wondered what it would feel like crushing his nose under my fist.

"I didn't think any pussy was worth one million dollars, but I can see why you went after that one."

A rush of anger rose to the surface before I could tame it. "Don't talk about what's mine."

The older man chuckled, as did his buddies next to him. "Or what?"

My lips twitched. He didn't know what he'd just walked into, but he was about to find out. "Remember Vern Tracey? All over the news a couple of years ago?"

"Yes, his body was never—"

His eyes widened as it all clicked into place.

I turned to face the stage again. "Glad we've reached an agreement."

He didn't bother turning back toward me and that was probably the best thing he'd done since he walked into this home. It was his best interest to shut the fuck up.

The auctions dragged on and when things finally came to an end, I stood up and walked out into the main hall. My attention turned to finding out any of the business dealings that were going down outside of this auction. No one was currently keeping tabs on me which made my job almost too easy. I studied some of the patrons and my surroundings, hoping to report more to Kingston.

Several guards were stationed in various sections of the house and with one standing by the staircase, I knew there was no way I was getting up there unless I was escorted by someone or caused a scene.

I debated placing bugs in Falcone's home, but I'd discovered that security was tight, especially for an event such as this, and would have been fruitless. When I arrived at the estate, my phone's signal slowly died, luckily after I sent a text to Kingston, so I knew that he had some sort of signal jammer in place.

I wandered down a hallway and found most of the doors closed, but I could hear a light murmuring coming from one of the rooms.

"Mr. Bolton?"

Shit. I turned and found the woman who'd escorted me to my seat earlier and interrupted the signing of the contract for my "prize." She looked as if she wished that I would have placed a bid on her.

"Can I help you with something?"

"No." I didn't bother defending myself because she wouldn't be able to prove what I was doing. If this wasn't a job from Will, I wouldn't give a shit if she'd figured out my true motives. Her eyes scanned my body a couple of times, making me think that she wished I would take her home.

"Are you ready to collect your purchase?"

I raised an eyebrow at the woman in front of me and I saw her quiver slightly.

"I'll take you to her."

She walked toward the main hallway that I'd entered when I arrived and then up a set of stairs. She led me down a long hallway and continued until we reached a door on the left. I'd expected her to knock on it, but instead she just opened the door.

I found the woman in red staring out the window on the opposite side of the room. She didn't move a muscle even when the woman cleared her throat.

"You'll be heading home tonight with Mr. Bolton here. If you fulfill your end of the bargain and Mr. Bolton has no complaints, then you can consider whatever you owe Mr. Falcone wiped clean. Do you understand me?"

Although she nodded her head slightly to show that she'd heard, she still didn't say anything.

"Take as much time as you need."

The guide excused herself, leaving me alone with the lady in red.

I took three steps into the room before I said, "Turn around. I want to see you."

She looked to her left but didn't turn to me.

"I said to turn around."

"You don't get to order me around."

Her voice was huskier than I expected, and I couldn't stop my mind from thinking about what it would sound like when I was fucking her.

"The amount of money that I just bid on you says otherwise," I said as I took another step forward.

She turned and faced the window again, hell-bent on defying me. My gut had told me that this might be fun, and I was glad to have trusted it.

"If you don't turn around by the time I count to three I'm going to give up this arrangement and tell Falcone I want my money back. One."

She didn't move an inch, but I knew my threat carried a lot of weight. I'm sure he held something over her head to force her to take part in the auction. She didn't want him to carry out whatever threat he made.

"Two."

It was a dirty shot, but it did the trick. Before I could say three, she whipped around quickly, the red fabric following the motions of her body.

Instead of the fear that I spotted in her eyes earlier, there was anger ready to be unleashed. Since there was nothing I could do to lessen the animosity that she felt toward me given the situation, I ran my finger along her shoulder and watched as she jerked back, but not before I saw the goose bumps appear on her flesh.

What had she done that had led her to borrow money from Falcone? I was determined to find out, even if right now wasn't the right time.

"My name is Ace. What's yours?"

It almost sounded comical coming from my lips, given what had just thrown us together.

"Harlow. It's Harlow."

I tossed her name around in my mind for a moment. "There are some things I need to wrap up here, but I'll come back and get you when it's time to leave."

11

HARLOW

I often thought that segments of my life just couldn't be real. Yet here I was sitting in the passenger seat of a Porsche Boxster after having been purchased by its driver. If I wrote a book about it, no one would believe me. I placed one hand into the other and gently squeezed, a habit I'd started when I was a child.

"Where are you from, besides Falcone's Bar 53?"

His deep voice dragged me out of the rabbit hole my mind had jumped down as I replayed what had occurred. He remembered seeing me a few days ago at my job. Well, my former job now if my debt was going to be cleared. I didn't have much of an answer because I didn't really belong anywhere. But that wasn't what I said to him.

"Is this your attempt at small talk?"

"It's one of the few things I'm not good at. Answer the question."

"All over," I answered, which wasn't a lie.

Bouncing between foster homes would do that to a person. The sternness in his voice fit him perfectly and sent a chill down my spine. Now that I was closer to him, I noticed some of the gray peeking through the scruff he had on his face, making me think he might have been older than I thought when I first saw him at Bar 53.

"How did you end up owing Falcone money?"

"What brought you to an auction where you decided it was a good idea to purchase a human?"

He cut his eyes over at me and I couldn't help but become giddy. Winning one over on him, however minor, sent a thrill through me different from the chill I'd just experienced. I hadn't felt like this since... forever. Something told me that based on the look in his eyes that I'd made the wrong decision. His brown eyes darkened considerably, and I wondered if the devil himself had appeared.

"Here are some ground rules—"

The slight daze I felt I'd been in for most of the day snapped. His words infuriated me, but I promised myself I would remain calm. "I'm not agreeing to anything you say."

"You don't have to agree, but you will obey, Sweetness."

That promise went out the window. I turned to look at him with a balled-up fist. Hitting him while he was driving could get us both killed, so I refrained. "The hell I will. And don't fucking call me that."

"But you will because I bought you and I intend to get my money's worth."

His predatory gaze danced over my face and dipped down to my chest before turning to focus on the road. I held on to my hands a bit tighter as thoughts of what he could mean by that coasted through my mind. It wasn't hard to infer what he meant, and I needed to grab the upper hand here.

"I want to have an agreement."

"Oh? Now you do? But just several seconds ago, I thought you said you weren't agreeing to anything?"

He had me there. "I didn't trust that the ground rules you were about to say would be beneficial to me in any way."

"That's smart because they weren't. I'm intrigued by where you're going with this. Continue."

I could hear him mocking me with his tone, but it didn't stop me. "I want a timeline on when all of this will end."

"All of this?"

"This arrangement between you and me. I assume that since you b-bought me at the auction, that the money I owed Falcone has officially been paid." Saying those words hurt my soul in a way I couldn't describe. Over the years, I thrived on thinking that I'd frozen any feelings that I might have had, due to how fucked up the world had been to me, but being bought and sold tonight had done a number on the walls I thought I'd built.

"Yes."

He was giving nothing away and I felt as if I was walking into a trap, but I had to keep going. "When will I be... free? To move on with my life?"

He didn't reply right away, and I didn't know if he was stalling because he didn't have an answer or because he wanted to cause even more panic within me. If I had to guess, it was the latter.

"What if I said you're never allowed to leave?"

My head jerked back, and it wasn't from being in a car. "There's no way you want me to stay with you forever. You'll get tired of me within hours."

He didn't reply and my thoughts began to spiral. There was no way he could keep me forever. I had hopes and dreams that I wanted to accomplish and a life to live, no matter how shitty my beginnings were.

"A month?" I asked.

"Three months."

I could survive three months. He wouldn't break me because I'd survived worse.

"I will be collecting every. Single. Thing. Make no mistake about that."

If his words did a terrible job at it, his tone and the look on his face indicated what he meant. The way he undressed me with his eyes before focusing on the road indicated what he meant. He wanted everything I could give him, including my body. "I'm not doing anything that I don't want to do."

"Of course not, because you're going to be pleading with me to take you. And there will never be anything more to this than just sex, got it?"

"You're fucking sick."

"Wouldn't be the first time I've heard that."

"And here I thought you weren't a monster."

This time he smiled, but it didn't give me any warm and fuzzy feelings.

"Whatever gave you that idea? If I wasn't, would I have been at the auction tonight?"

I was beginning to question whether I was right about this man being my savior from this debacle. The longer I spent in his presence, the more I was beginning to think I was wrong.

The three months that Ace said I would have to stay with him was feeling longer by the moment. Doubt crept in, making me wonder if I could survive this. I didn't know this man at all, and his dark brown eyes hid many secrets behind them. I shouldn't be drawn to him because while he'd saved me from dealing with Ian and Falcone, I didn't trust him. He was still perpetuating the same system that allowed me to be sold to him in the first place. Was he much different than those two?

I doubted it.

WHEN WE DROVE up to a set of gates, my immediate thoughts drifted back to how quickly my life had changed when I was driven up to another set of gates just hours before. Ace stopped the car and glanced at a man standing nearby, who then must have pressed a button to open the gates to his estate. Soon we were driving up the driveway not too dissimilar from the home we'd just left.

Ace opened the front door and when we walked inside, I couldn't stop myself from staring at the home around me. I'd learn to judge people to survive, but if I had to guess what Ace's home would look like, it wasn't this.

"Mr. Bolton."

Both Ace and I turned, and I found an older man staring back at me.

"Harlow, this is Anderson. Anderson, Harlow. She's the one that I said would be staying with us for the foreseeable future."

"Ah, yes, Sir."

"Will you please show her where she'll be staying?"

Without a glance toward me, Ace walked away as if he'd just dropped off a package with his butler and expected him to take care of everything.

In a way, I was a package. Just a thing that he bought and picked up off the street and forced to be his.

"Come this way, Ms. Harlow."

Having someone call me "Ms." was foreign to my ears. I'd been called plenty of names, many unsavory and filled with hate, in my life. But the small amount of niceness and respect that Anderson had shown me in the seconds since I'd arrived meant more than I could have ever thought.

Anderson gave me a quick tour of the home, including a look at Ace's extensive car collection. Although Anderson seemed friendly enough, this home was the exact opposite. I would even say that the house was creepy. The house was dated and the dark choices in paint and furniture looked like it would be better suited for a horror movie than someone who was willing to throw away one million dollars on a whim. It wasn't until he showed me the library that I felt a small sense of calm around me.

I'd always been able to lose myself in a book and this library had so many books that I'm sure I could find something to read here. We stayed in the library a bit longer than the other locations he stopped in, but I was also pleased to find a pool attached to the home. It had an enclosure over it, and I couldn't wait to go swimming at some point during my stay here. At least there were a couple of things to look forward to while I was here.

Anderson led me upstairs and down a hallway in silence, allowing me to be with my thoughts. I was happy to be away from Ace after the drive we'd shared. Although we'd only known each other for maybe four hours, he took up all the oxygen whenever I was near him. I didn't know much about what my life would be like here, but having him away from me even temporarily gave me the ability to breathe.

Anderson stopped at a door and turned the knob. I followed him into the room.

"I get my own room?" I controlled the urge to sigh with relief at not having to share a room with Ace.

"Yes, miss. Mr. Bolton requested that you have this room." Anderson walked farther into the room and pointed to a closed door. "His bedroom is right through that door."

My relief was short-lived. He'd chosen the room that was adjacent to his for me to sleep in, probably so that he could have easy access to me without having to step into the hall.

I intend to get my money's worth.

Those words would haunt me. When he said them, I felt them in every inch of my mind, body, and soul, and I knew that he would have no issue with coming to collect.

"Everything that you need should be in here and in the bathroom. We have the basics and the rest of the things that Mr. Bolton ordered should be here by tomorrow morning."

"I don't want anything that Mr. Bolton ordered," I snapped. I was impressed that given that only a few hours had passed since the contract had been signed with Falcone he'd done all of this.

Anderson shrugged, and I could feel my cheeks growing hot.

"I'm sorry, I shouldn't have said that." After all, he was just following orders from the asshole himself.

"Not to worry. Your things from your apartment will also be here in the morning."

All thoughts of apologizing flew out of my mind just as quickly as they'd arrived. "I can get my things—"

Anderson smiled at me briefly. "It's already been taken care of. Is there anything I can get you?"

I shook my head and watched as he left my room, closing my door behind him. I stared at the closed door for a moment before a deep timbre cut through my thoughts.

"Is everything to your liking?"

I gasped and spun around. I found Ace standing behind me, and it was clear that he'd walked in through the door connecting our rooms. How hadn't I heard him? Or felt him suck the air out of the room?

"You'll answer me when I ask you a question. Is everything to your liking?"

I nodded, not trusting myself to respond. I grew increasingly pissed and wanted to lash out, but what would that get me in the long run? I needed to play this smart for as long as I could.

"Good. And if you need anything else, Anderson is the person to go to. There's also Marnie, my chef, who might be of help in certain instances too. Speaking of the chef, dinner will be served in thirty minutes, and I expect you to be down there. The clothes that you are to wear have been placed in the bathroom."

"I can pick out my own fucking clothes." I turned my back to him and clenched my fists. My hands were so tight that I was sure I would draw blood.

"I know you can, but it wasn't required. Your outfit has been selected for you, and I will see you downstairs when dinner is served."

"I'm not wearing anything you picked. Chances are it's some scant little thing. Leave."

"Harlow, you're in my home and living under my rules. I'll

leave when I choose to, not when you decide. Remember that and maybe you'll make it out of this unscathed. Dinner will be served in twenty-nine minutes, and I expect that you'll be down to join me."

"You have some fucking—" Playing it smart was thrown out in the same way that my patience had been.

I whipped around and found that I was talking to myself. That further enraged me, and I slammed the door that connected our two rooms shut.

12

ACE

I looked over my shoulder and stared at the closed door. I adjusted my jaw before I ate up the distance between me and the door and yanked it open.

Harlow twirled around and her eyes widened. Good, I'd surprised her.

"Don't ever slam a door in my home. Got it?"

She took a step toward me. "Don't treat me like I'm a toddler."

"Well, when you're acting like one—"

She made a motion as if she was going to slap me before I grabbed her wrist and held on tightly. When she winced, I loosened my grip a smidge, letting her know that I wouldn't physically hurt her, but that I wouldn't tolerate her hitting me. The potential to hurt her emotionally was a different matter altogether.

"Breaking you is going to be one of the most thrilling adventures of my life and I'll enjoy every moment of it."

Her eyes widened before she caught herself. Soon they

narrowed into a glare. Watching the fire grow in her eyes was a turn-on, something I hadn't felt in a long time.

"You wouldn't dare."

"Continue to try me and—"

She took a step toward me and said, "And you'll what?"

Instead of responding to her, I walked out of the room, letting her think she'd won. I closed the door connecting our rooms behind me, having already set that door to lock automatically. I walked over to my dresser, grabbed a key, and then left my bedroom and walked out into the hallway and locked her bedroom door from the outside.

"What the—" I heard her muffled voice say before she turned the doorknob. When she realized I had, indeed, locked it, she gasped before what I assumed was her fists hit the door. "Ace! Let me out!"

"Welcome to your first lesson. When you earn the privilege to freely walk around my home, you shall do so."

Without another word, I turned away, leaving her to shout and bang on the door for as long as she wanted. I made a note to tell Anderson to be careful when he came upstairs to serve her dinner. I'd debated having him call her down for dinner but figured that some time apart might help her to calm down.

This whole thing could have been avoided if I'd let her go. It would have been easy to do so. The million that I paid Falcone wouldn't have been missed and I could have let her go and drove her back to New York City. But I didn't.

Because I was taught that money doesn't save people. Only they can save themselves.

I walked into my office and shut the door behind me. As I sat down in my chair, I thought about everything that had happened over the last few hours. This might have been the biggest one-eighty that my life had taken since I made it my mission in life to inflict revenge on Kiki. Or when I found out that my rich grandfather had named his bastard grandson as the heir to his empire.

When my phone vibrated on my desk, I glanced over to check the notification, and I wasn't surprised to see the number on the screen. I didn't bother with hello when I answered the phone.

"Did you get any information from the Falcone party?"

"I did. The whole premise behind the party was that he's auctioning women off to the highest bidder. There might be some other shit going down there too, but that I couldn't confirm without raising eyebrows."

"That's a start, then. I don't think Will is in the game of auctioning people off though."

I quickly debated with myself about whether I should tell him about Harlow before deciding that I needed to. "I ended up bidding on someone... for one million dollars."

He didn't respond right away, and I knew what the next thing out of his mouth would be. "What the hell were you thinking?"

"Kingston..."

"Man, I'm serious. What the hell were you thinking bidding on a woman for one million dollars?"

I'd asked myself the same question a million times since I raised my paddle in the air. "It's not your money, so why the fuck are you concerned about it?"

"Because that wasn't the point of you being there and now you've become a liability. You aren't thinking clearly and—"

"What the fuck do you mean? I saved her from being some older man's piece of ass."

"And you're so much better? Ace, I know you better than most people. Can you honestly say that you're much better than any of those other fuckers that I assume were there?"

Deep down, I knew that he was right. I was too damaged, too fucked up. I shouldn't willingly bring anyone into my world, for they were guaranteed to not make it out alive. Yet I did. Because it was her.

There was a pull that I'd never felt before, and I gravitated toward her the moment I stepped into the room and she to the stage. And I wouldn't be denied.

"But this also gets me on Falcone's good side. He mentioned getting me involved in some of his other businesses. Trust me on this, okay?"

I'd never given Kingston an opportunity not to trust me and this time shouldn't be any different.

"How long are you requiring her to stay with you?" His accusatory tone dimmed to a slightly more friendly one.

"I told her three months." I let the lie pass my lips without a second thought. I wasn't ready to admit to anyone that I had no intention of letting her leave me.

"I assume she didn't react too kindly to that."

"She didn't have much of a choice."

Kingston sighed. "This isn't like you, Ace."

I shrugged even though he couldn't see me. "Maybe I'm turning over a new leaf."

"Bullshit. You don't do things spur of the moment. You spend a lot of time plotting, calculating, being an asshole and—"

"Thanks. I'll take it as a compliment."

"Of course you would." Kingston paused, I assumed, to gather his thoughts. "None of this impacted what you found while there, so on the business side of things I don't care what you do. But I'm not going to say I'm not worried about you personally. After all that you've gone through..."

I rubbed a hand across my face. "I understand your concern, but I'm fine. Let me know what else you need me to do to get this taken care of for Will."

"It's going to require you going away for a few days. Are you all right with that given your new 'situation'?"

I thought about Harlow briefly before I pushed her out of my mind. I was determined to show that her being here had no impact on what I was doing. "Of course I am. Where am I going?"

LATER THAT EVENING, Kingston's words ran through my mind as I walked down the hallway. He was right. Although I'd completed what I was tasked with, I came home with something I shouldn't have, probably further complicating matters, but I couldn't care less. If Falcone knew I was there on behalf of Will DePalma, shit was going to hit the fan, and I'd be forced to deal with him.

I opened the door to Harlow's room and peered inside. The moonlight shone into the room in such a way that I was able to make out her face.

She shifted her body and I watched as her face furrowed. Even in sleep, she couldn't rest peacefully.

What happened to you?

She twisted her body in such a way that once she settled,

her face was hidden from view, something that irritated me. I walked across the threshold and into her room, determined to see her one last time before I too fell into a restless sleep.

Once I reached the bed, I couldn't stop myself from sweeping a lock of hair back so I could see her face in all of its glory.

When it seemed as if she'd settled down, I walked back over to the door and turned around to stare at her delicate body before I closed the door softly behind me.

She'd come to me.

She'd be mine.

13

HARLOW

My eyes popped open, and I saw the moon casting a small beam of light through the curtains. I'd lost count of how many times I'd woken up now and not having a phone meant I had no way of knowing what time it was.

I wondered what had woken me up this time. Was it a strange noise or just being in an unfamiliar place? I'd always had a hard time adjusting to a new bed, and once I'd grown comfortable in one, I would have to give it up and move to another home with another family and you never knew what you were going to get.

This wasn't much different from what I was feeling right now. Only this time, I wasn't a little girl anymore. Still, the ever-present feeling of fear was near because I didn't know what being here would bring me... or do to me.

I curled my body up into the fetal position, willing myself to fall back to sleep.

I'd spent the rest of the evening locked away in this bedroom. I debated banging on the door that connected our rooms, but thought better of it because it might give him a hard-on. I got the feeling he'd love to hear me beg for him to open the door.

Exhaustion had swept through my weary body. With everything that had happened yesterday, I'd still fallen into a restless sleep and woken up several times throughout the night.

I wrapped the comforter on the bed around myself again and fell into a dreamless sleep.

I EXPLORED my room for what felt like the millionth time and groaned in frustration. It felt as if I was stuck in a cage. Since Ace had locked me in this bedroom, I'd been staring at these four walls outside of watching television and getting served meals as often as I wanted. It was like staying in a hotel, but without the ability to come and go as I wanted. There was also the fact that I was sleeping next door to a deranged asshole who took great pride and joy in making me suffer.

Someone knocked on the door and I responded in kind. I got the feeling that it couldn't be Ace because he seemed as if he was the type of person who didn't give a shit about knocking before entering a room, especially in his own home. I wasn't surprised to see Anderson open the door. Ace couldn't even bear to face me after he locked me in a bedroom overnight.

"Where is Ace?" I asked before he had a chance to greet me.

"He's not at the residence currently, but he'll be back soon. Did you want anything for lunch?"

He's not here?

"No, he had business in the city."

I didn't realize I'd asked the question out loud. Why did I care if he was here or not? Him not being here was a good thing.

When he walked over to the door, he turned back to me and asked, "Do you want to leave the door open or closed?"

I cleared my throat. "I have a choice?"

"Yes. Mr. Bolton thought it would be fine to leave the door unlocked."

That sentence was enough to make me see red. "Well, you can tell 'Mr. Bolton' that he can... tell me all of this himself."

I changed my tactic because I shouldn't take my anger out on Anderson. He was just following orders from the asshole in charge.

"That reminds me," Anderson said as he reached into his pocket. What he pulled out left me befuddled.

"This is a smartphone. A very expensive smartphone."

I felt like an idiot as the words fell from my mouth like boulders charging down a hill.

"And it's yours. Mr. Bolton had it delivered this morning. All of your contacts were transferred over to this one."

That would mean a quick turnaround, given that I'd just arrived here last night. Unless he was already planning on bidding on someone last night...

"He didn't need to buy me a phone. My old one worked just fine."

"I assume he wanted to because since I've known him, he hasn't done anything that he doesn't want to do."

"Where is my old phone?"

"It wasn't returned with this one."

I knew that was his way of saying it had been thrown away. I shivered as I took the phone from his outstretched hand. I'd never been able to afford a smartphone, and I never felt the need to have one when a cheaper phone would suffice. Now I had one hand delivered to me.

"The phone is set up for you to use immediately and your things should be here—"

His words were cut off when the doorbell rang. The tune was both lovely, yet creepy at the same time.

"Right now. I'll bring everything upstairs."

"How did Ace know where I lived to be able to retrieve my things?"

This time, Anderson gave a small smile. "Mr. Bolton has his ways. I'll be right back."

Before I could ask another question, Anderson was gone, and I was left dumbfounded at what had just transpired.

As I closed the drawer that held the last of my clothes, I couldn't help but feel even more out of place even with my things in the room. It was clear that my clothes, old laptop that had been gifted to me, and all of my other secondhand items didn't belong in a place like this.

Once I'd finished unpacking and thought that Anderson wasn't coming back, I sent a text to Emma.

Me: *Hey, I just want to let you know that I'm okay. I know it's been a few days since we've seen each other.*

Instead of sending me a message back, my phone rang, and I smiled when I saw her name pop up on the screen. "Harlow, I've been so worried about you. Where are you?"

I thought about everything that had happened since I'd last seen her, and I didn't know where to begin. "Long story short, Ian ratted me out and now I'm doing something else to pay off the debt I owe Falcone."

"You've got to be kidding me," she said. "How bad is it?"

"Depends on your definition of the word *bad*." Yes, I didn't have to work at the bar anymore, but I was convinced that Ace was more dangerous than anyone I'd encountered there.

"Harlow..."

"I'm fine. I know what I'm doing."

"Fuck..." Her voice faded out and I heard some rustling in the background. "I'm just happy to hear your voice. I was worried he'd killed you or something."

She made me feel guilty. "I'm sorry. I should have found a way to reach out sooner, but I didn't have a phone until now." I took a deep breath. "How are things at the bar?"

"Okay. Ian has an even bigger stick up his ass since you've been gone."

"You'd think he'd have removed it since I'm not there anymore."

"I'm not sure what's up with him, and I try not to hang around him long, so I haven't been able to find out."

Understandable. "Is he leaving you alone?"

"He—" Emma paused for so long that I almost wondered if she'd hung up. "Yeah, he is. At least for now."

It was good that he was keeping the peace for now.

"Harlow?"

"Yes?"

"If you need to get out of... wherever you are, please let me know. I'll do everything I can to help you."

"Thank—"

A knock on the window made me jump. I walked over to it to see if I could see anything outside, but I couldn't.

"Listen, I'll talk to you later." My words came out rushed and much quieter than I had been talking.

"Yes, keep me posted. And I'm serious. If there is anything I can do…"

The thought that she wanted to help me, warmed my heart. I knew there was no way she had any means to get me out of this, but I appreciated the sentiment. We both knew that there was nothing she could do outside of finding a way to pay off what I owed. And if she were to come up with the money, I expected her to pay her debt off first.

I hung up the phone and looked at the window once again. I pulled it open and stuck my head outside. It reminded me of how I contemplated escaping at Falcone's place before that window of opportunity closed. While I might have contemplated jumping out of that window, there was no way I was going to make it out of this one without seriously injuring or killing myself.

I leveraged all my weight and pushed the window until it was closed.

I opened the door and peeked out into the hallway. Thankfully no one was there, and I slipped out of my room. The eerie silence that greeted me as I walked down the hall was all but welcoming.

Once I slowly closed the door, I walked down the hallway with no objective in mind other than getting out of this bedroom after being stuck there for hours. The time that I'd been locked in there had taken its toll and I was determined to get out even if it meant just walking around the house.

I had no idea where I was going, allowing my feet to lead

me wherever they saw fit. Before long, I ended up standing in front of a heavy wooden door. I'd taken a wrong turn before I wandered into the library that Anderson had shown me when he was giving me a tour of the home. Whenever things got tough, getting lost in a good book helped me hide from my pain.

With a slight creak, the door opened, and I found a light switch that illuminated the entire space. Although this was the second time that I'd seen the library, I was still amazed by how many books were there. It would be easy to get lost in here with a good novel.

I walked over to one of the shelves and pulled out a thick book. A wave of dust came with it, and I did my best not to sneeze. When I steadied my nose, I ran my fingers across the title on the cover. It was a shame that something so precious had just been sitting here collecting dust.

I found what I hoped was a comfortable chair in the corner near a window that looked out at the vast lands of the estate and dug into the book. I knew that if it was a good one it would keep me occupied for hours.

"Ms. Robinson."

I jumped and turned my head as if I'd been caught doing something I shouldn't be. What was up with people in this house sneaking around? And when was the last time anyone had called me by my last name? Mama Robinson briefly appeared in my head before I buried thoughts of her away. This was not the time for that baggage.

"I'm not surprised to find you here after your interest in the library during the tour."

"I assumed it was okay that I was down here... or would Ace have a problem with me sitting here and minding my business?" I said unapologetically. If he had a problem with me reading a book...

"No, you can read as many books as you wish. I wanted to tell you that lunch would be served soon."

I knew I sounded overly defensive, but there was no taking it back now.

"Uh, thank you. I'll be up shortly. Thanks."

"You're welcome."

He turned and walked away while I was left staring at the empty space he left in his wake.

I looked back out the window.

Just under three months until I get out of here.

14

HARLOW

I awoke with a start once again, my heart pounding as I looked around the room I was in.

Fuck.

This was the second time it had happened in the three days I'd been in this home I referred to as a prison.

Should I be calling this a prison since it's the nicest place I've ever slept in? Probably not, but it felt like such.

I still hadn't seen Ace since he locked me in this guest room. It would be a lie if I said I hadn't been lulled into a sense of security that I knew I shouldn't be in. I wasn't safe here, just like I wasn't safe anywhere.

I lay back down in bed, hopeful that I would get back to sleep as soon as possible. I heard a loud noise from Ace's bedroom, and it made me jump. It was the last thing I needed with my heart already beating a thousand miles per hour. I waited to see if another sound would come from the room, but there was none. I debated exploring further, but it was none of my business. Plus, I didn't want to face Ace this late at night because who knew what that would lead to?

When I settled back into bed, I heard the door closest to me crack open. My heart was beating faster than a jackhammer pounding away on a New York City street. My eyes snapped shut and I pretended that I was asleep, but I couldn't help but wonder if he could hear my heart beating due to how loud it was in my ears.

I heard a creak come from the wooden floor, and given how many times I'd paced this room, I had a good idea of where he was standing. If he was where I thought, he was still several feet away. Was he just staring at me lying in bed? What the hell for? Was he thinking about getting into bed with me?

But he didn't.

I heard another creak, and then the door between our rooms closed lightly, putting a barrier between us again. When I knew for sure that he wasn't coming back, I finally took a breath.

"Mr. Bolton requests your presence at dinner."

It was later the next day when I looked up from my phone and found Anderson standing in the doorway of my bedroom. When he walked up, I didn't know.

"And he couldn't tell me himself?" I closed my eyes and took a deep breath as soon as the last word left my mouth. Once again, I had to remind myself that Anderson wasn't Ace, although due to his employment, he was an extension of him. Yet, I still hadn't wanted to take my anger out on him. After all, he wasn't the reason I was here.

His expression said nothing. "He had to run an errand but

should return in approximately twenty-five minutes. He also requested that you wear one of the dresses that is currently in the closet."

The way he said it nonchalantly felt as if he'd done this a million times before.

"How many other women have had to do this same crap?" I asked before I could stop myself. Why did I care who else had been here? It didn't matter in my grand plan.

"No one. You're the only woman Mr. Bolton has brought back here since he moved in."

"And when was that?" I just couldn't stop myself from asking questions apparently.

"About four years ago, miss."

So, he hadn't lived here all that long, but it was long enough to renovate the home if he chose to. Why hadn't he?

"I'll be down shortly," I said and gave Anderson a small smile before he left me alone once more. I hadn't paid much attention to the clothes in the closet when I was putting my things away, because it wasn't mine. If what Anderson said was true, why was there a closet full of women's clothes in here?

I opened the closet and began to touch what could only be described as what felt like a clothing rack at one of the most expensive clothing stores that New York City offered. The ripped jeans and T-shirt that I got secondhand were in a different world compared to what was in this closet. I found the red dress that I wore at the auction. I stared at it for a moment before I moved the hanger to the side.

I pulled out a black dress that caught my attention and my eyes migrated toward the tag. They nearly bulged out of my skull.

"You've got to be shitting me..." I mumbled as I stared at the price. How could this dress cost thousands of dollars? I couldn't possibly wear this ever because it wasn't me.

Should I play a role and suck it up for as long as I had to be here? I shook my head at myself. When had I ever just given up, instead of fighting for what I wanted or needed?

I tossed the black dress back in the closet, deciding that my jeans, T-shirt, and ratty sneakers would have to do. I could bother brushing my hair, so I walked into the bathroom and took out my messy bun. I grabbed my old brush that I'd had for years and swept it through my hair. Being able to do something that was a part of my routine in this unfamiliar environment gave me a boost of energy and defiance.

When I was finished, I still had some time to waste and walked out of the bathroom and to my laptop that Anderson had so kindly left for me on the desk. They'd even brought over the picture of Mama Robinson that I'd placed next to my laptop on the desk. Having her photo here forced complicated feelings to grow within me. I felt that she would be proud of me for persevering, but look at the mess I had gotten myself into as a result. I turned her picture away from me slightly and opened the laptop. I found a Post-it from what I assumed was Anderson with the Wi-Fi information on it. His neat handwriting matched the proper demeanor that he had on display every time I'd interacted with him.

While I waited for my laptop to boot up, I decided that I would try to do some research on Ace. I figured using my laptop might be safer than the new phone he'd purchased. Then again, there was a chance that he'd put some sort of tracker on my laptop without my knowledge. I didn't put anything past him, but I was determined to find out at least something about him. I knew nothing about the man who barely seemed to live in this gigantic home, and something in his background might help me to survive. Ace Bolton couldn't be too common of a name.

A few clicks on several websites didn't provide much information outside of some key points about his life. His mother died when he was young, and it seemed as if his father wasn't in the picture because he wasn't mentioned anywhere. That was where his story ended. I scrolled back up and reread a section of the website.

Ace inherited what looked to be this home and his grandfather's multitude of businesses in various industries. The timing of when this occurred lined up with what Anderson said. It would also explain the dated look that the home had, but what it didn't tell me was why Ace hadn't bothered to update the interior of the home to make it less old-fashioned. He was now worth billions of dollars, had enough money to spend on clothes that he would never wear, but didn't bother removing some of the wallpaper in here that was from several decades ago.

The rest of my search didn't provide any more information than that, which was a bummer. Outside of the brief mention of his childhood and how he came to live in this home, Ace remained an enigma, and I was still in the dark. The decor of the home and his personality made him scarier. Although he'd done nothing to harm me yet, I couldn't fight the feeling that it was only a matter of time.

I looked at the clock on my screen and realized that Ace should be here at any moment. I closed the web browser and stood up from my seat. With light steps, I walked over to the door and listened for him coming in. When I heard nothing, I debated whether I wanted to go downstairs to have dinner with him to begin with. When my stomach grumbled, I had my answer, and I walked down the hallway and down the stairs to the main floor.

I'd hoped I beat him to the dining room, to give me some grace before I had to see him, but my research had led me to be later than intended because he was already seated at the head of the table.

"That doesn't look like a dress," he said without looking up at me as I entered the room.

"No shit," I replied. "Glad to see you can tell the difference between articles of clothing."

"Sit down next to me."

"I rather sit across from you." I didn't know what he would do to me if I was sitting mere inches from him.

"I didn't ask what you would rather do. I told you what to do."

His voice grew deeper, and he looked up at me this time. From here, his eyes looked like black orbs, ready to suck me in whole and force me to do whatever he wanted.

"Come here."

There was no room for arguing this time. His words had a finality to them that brought up a memory of one of my foster parents. I'd vowed to keep that memory buried in the back of my mind forever, but I failed. My body had a mind of its own as I walked over and when I was within a few feet of him, he stood up and looked down at me.

He raised an eyebrow and I saw a glimpse of confusion in his eyes that quickly disappeared. His eyes looked even more haunting up close. Before I could react, he wrapped his hand around my hair and pulled back, not hurting me, but forcing me to look up at him.

"I can't wait to have you in a similar position while I'm coming all over your face."

I pulled against him, but his grip kept me in my current position. He used his other hand to lightly rub my cheek and I shivered at his touch. I'd hoped he hadn't noticed, but when he smirked, it was clear that he had.

"Now, sit to my left and let's enjoy a meal together."

With that, he let me go and I was left momentarily stunned, staring at him in shock before doing as he said. In the back of my mind, I knew I needed to tread lightly even if all I wanted to do was to tell Ace to go to hell and walk out of here. Because the only other option meant that I would have to return to Falcone.

I knew he had no intention of letting me come back to work at the bar, because now I would have cost him the money I owed him, plus the extra money that Ace bought me for. If I returned to Falcone and he was forced to pay Ace back, I was better off dead.

15

ACE

I shouldn't have touched her, but I couldn't help myself. Seeing the fire in her eyes did something to me. Even now, my dick was hardening at the thought. I wanted her body to show me just how much I'd pissed her off.

Marnie came into the room just as Harlow sat down to my right because of course she doesn't listen.

"Harlow, this is Marnie. Marnie, this is Harlow."

Only then did Harlow shake off the dazed look in her eyes and bestow a small smile at the woman standing next to her.

"Mr. Bolton asked that I whip something up quick, so here's what we have. If you want something else, I'd be happy to make it for you." Marnie glanced at me out of the corner of her eye as she spoke, and I knew why. She knew what I liked, but I hadn't given her any information regarding Harlow's dietary restrictions.

"Oh no, this looks fantastic. Thank you so much," Harlow responded, her eyes darting between the food and Marnie. She was avoiding looking at me, and after what had just occurred between the two of us, I didn't blame her.

"That will be all, Marnie."

Marnie looked at me and nodded before she left the room, closing the dining room door behind her. I picked up my fork and looked at Harlow. I leaned back slightly and found that she was holding her hands in her lap, much like she had while I was signing the paperwork to make her mine. This seemed to be a comforting habit for her.

When I started digging into my food, something struck me as strange.

"Harlow." This time she looked at me, and something about her eyes hit me in the gut. "You can start eating your food."

I didn't expect to have to tell her she could eat, but she took that as permission and slowly cut into the steak she'd been served.

"Uh—I was daydreaming," she said.

I didn't believe her.

I watched as she took the piece of meat and placed it lightly in her mouth. Once she started chewing, her eyes drifted closed and a small moan left her lips.

"Good?" I asked as I too cut into my steak and stole a glimpse at her. A slight blush fell onto her cheeks, a clear indicator that she hadn't meant to moan out loud. I filed that she loved steak away in my mind.

"It's delicious. Marnie did a fantastic job with it and the sides."

"She's a wonderful cook. You won't have to worry about anything food-related if it's coming from her. If you want something during the day you can just let her, or Anderson know."

"I don't want to be a bother," she said.

The way she said it made me look up from my own plate. "Who told you that you were a bother?"

Harlow stopped moving and her eyes slowly made their way to mine. "I got told that a lot in foster care."

I watched as her eyes drifted back down to her plate. The only sound that could be heard between us was the sound of cutlery swirling around on our dinner plates, neither one of us making the effort to finish our food. This wasn't what I had been expecting her to say, but I recovered quickly.

"It won't be any trouble, I swear."

Harlow nodded and then patted her lips to remove the crumbs from them. I couldn't help but stare. Her admission and willingness to be vulnerable even for a split second was a turn-on. It made me want to peel back the rest of her layers and break down the walls that she'd built up around her, but that could never be. I didn't want to share my deepest, darkest secrets in return and see judgment in her eyes.

Instead, I chose to focus on her lips, which she'd just briefly licked. They were begging to be taken, and I couldn't remove the image of her wrapping her mouth around my cock from my mind. One of those things was much more likely to happen than the other, whether she knew it or not.

"There is something I'd like to talk about."

"Okay."

"I want to discuss our arrangement."

That shifted the mood in the room. I put my fork down and wiped my mouth with a cloth napkin. "This sounds like you want to negotiate the terms that were agreed upon."

She nodded. "I do."

"You do realize you have no leverage here," I said matter-of-factly. It was the truth. The agreement that I had made with Falcone was between him and me, in exchange for paying off the debt she owed him, she'd become mine to do whatever I want with.

"I know, but I thought you would be a reasonable person and we could talk about this."

"Whatever gave you the idea that I was reasonable?"

I watched as she took this in and swallowed hard. I was telling the truth, and a slight irritation rose in me that she was trying to bargain with me when she knew this would be a losing battle. But I had to admit, the fact that she was trying to reason with me when she held no leverage was admirable. Or maybe it was foolish.

"This ends after three months, right?"

"That is correct."

"And at the end of the three months, I'm free to do whatever I want."

"Yes." Why was she rehashing things we both already knew?

"And Falcone won't come after me. I'm repeating this to make sure that everything is clear."

"He won't because he's been paid in full by me. Why don't you tell me what you really want to discuss?"

"If you force me—"

I cut her off before she could continue. "I'm not going to force you to do anything you don't want to do, Harlow."

She looked at the dining room door before she whispered, "So sex is off the table."

I leaned forward, both elbows on the surface, and crossed my arms. I stared at her face, determined to make her look into my eyes and tell me that she didn't want to be fucked, but she refused to look at me. "It can be *on* the table if I so choose."

"I don't want to have sex with you at all. Anywhere, anytime, or anyplace."

I shrugged. "If you want to lie to yourself, please continue to do so."

"I'm not lying to myself or you."

"Harlow, now you have to look at this from my perspective as well. I didn't spend a million dollars just for you to move in here and eat dinner with me."

"Why did you bid on me then?"

I said the first thing that came to mind. "Because I wanted to rip that red dress off of you while you were on that stage and fuck you right there in front of everyone. And I meant it when I told you I intend to get my money's worth, because I refuse to waste a single dime of my purchase."

In one sweeping motion, I pulled her chair closer, and my hand landed on her thigh. Her eyes darted to the dining room door again before landing on mine. Interest and wonder lay in them before she closed them and looked down at the connection we shared. Her breath quickened slightly. She could deny it all she wanted, but her body didn't.

"Look, I just want to get this all over with and—"

"Including the sex you just mentioned you didn't want to have?" My hand moved up and down the seam of her jeans. If she'd done as I said, it would have been easy for me to finger her right now and to enjoy her for dessert. "Next time I tell you to wear something, you do it, got it? I'm letting a few things go right now because this is new for you, but my patience is wearing thin."

The redness in her cheeks this time had nothing to do

with her anger. The spark that I saw in her eyes almost every time we'd been in each other's presence was back and ready to ignite. She tossed my hand from her body.

I used the hand she pushed away to pick up my fork and I took one final bite of my dinner, slowly chewing before I swallowed the last of it. "You know what? Fucking you will be an absolute pleasure."

"Everything isn't about sex."

"And that's where you're wrong again. When it comes to this arrangement, that's all this is about."

16

———

HARLOW

The next day, I found myself still angry at how the conversation with Ace went down. I tied my hair up into a messy bun on the top of my head and sighed. Although I'd been given free rein of the place, I couldn't help but feel like Ace had just lengthened the leash I'd been put on because I was still trapped here.

I watched myself in the mirror and while the bruises had begun to fade, my lack of sleep last night was evident on my face. Hopefully that would change over the course of my stay here. The scratch on my shoulder was turning into a scar and hopefully, with time, it too would go away. After playing with my phone last night, I figured out how to use most of its basic functions and maybe it would be something I would be able to keep when I was free to go and live my life however I saw fit.

Still I had to make it out of this situation unscathed.

No more debt. I won't owe anything to anyone.

As I applied the makeup that would cover the discoloration that marked my skin, I fantasized about what life would be like not owing anything to anyone. It brought relief. Although I enjoyed living in New York City, maybe I'd move someplace else and start fresh. Getting through these next few months would provide that and I'd have time to figure out my next steps while I'm here. Maybe I could think more about pursuing my dream of owning a bookshop.

Speaking of letting it go, I needed to get out of this house, or I was going to lose my shit. Being stuck here was driving me mad, especially when I couldn't help but wonder when he was coming to collect. For someone who seemed to think about only sex when it came to me, he never tried to initiate anything, which made me wonder what game he was playing. After all, I was convinced that's all this was to him anyway.

I walked out of the bathroom, and my eyes landed on a photo of Mama Robinson. When my things were delivered, I was relieved to find that it had been included as well as a few of my books. Having them with me made things slightly easier because they were familiar. I glanced at the items once more before walking out of my room.

Anderson hadn't mentioned that Ace had left recently so I suspected he was intentionally avoiding me, which would have been fine by me if it hadn't been for him planting the seed of him wanting me on every surface of this house. As I walked through his home, I thought about the million different ways this conversation could go before stopping outside of a large wooden door. This avoidance game that he was playing would all come to an end right now, as I set my shoulders back and walked into what I'd found out was his office.

"Knock when you enter my office," he said without looking up at me.

"When you start to knock before you enter my bedroom, then I'll do the same for you."

He looked up from his desk and his lip twitched. One might even say he had a slight smile on his face. "Self-preservation eludes you at every corner, doesn't it?"

"What—" I rolled my eyes when I realized he was referring to our encounter in the dining room the evening before. "Kiss my ass."

What left his mouth after that shocked me. Ace Bolton chuckled at what I said. His laughter transformed his entire face into something I hadn't witnessed before. It was jarring, to say the least.

"Is there something that you want? You're racking up strikes every time you do something that you're not supposed to do. It seems that locking you in the bedroom did nothing."

"First, we haven't talked about what happened at dinner last night."

"What's there to talk about? Unless you want to take things further?"

I froze for a moment as I felt a slight fluttering in my belly. "Of course not."

It was a lie, but I'd be damned if I ever admitted the truth to him.

He leaned back in his chair and said, "You're lying, and we both know that you are."

This was getting nowhere. "Forget I said anything about it because this is a waste of time."

He shrugged but didn't offer a response. I waited a beat before I asked the second thing that had been on my mind.

"Can I at least have access to a car in case I want to drive into town? It would be nice to get out of the house."

I'd gotten a handle on how to operate my new smartphone and knew that I would have no problem getting to and from town by using my maps app.

He slowly rose from his chair and said, "You're right, getting out of the house would be nice for you." He paused and then said, "There is something you could do for me that might make me consider it."

His dark stare danced over my body, alluding to what he wanted. Was another inch of freedom worth whatever he had planned? Of course it was, but one thing frightened me. What if I enjoyed whatever he wanted me to do?

"What is it?" I licked my lips as I waited for his response.

His eyes followed my tongue's movements before he said, "You can get on your knees and put your lips around my cock. I've been daydreaming about that since last night."

"You must be kidding."

"Does anything on my face show that I'm making a joke?"

It didn't. The dark look that crossed his face was the exact opposite of the laughter he'd released only moments ago.

My run-in with Ian briefly flashed in my mind. I'd pushed that encounter to the far corners of my mind. But this felt different. Although he issued the order and I felt as if the tables had shifted slightly. If I did what he wanted me to do, I would be the one in control of him.

"Unzip my pants, Sweetness."

His words shut down any thoughts I had. The look in his eyes both frightened me and excited me. I swallowed hard again as I bent down in front of him, him looking like a king on a throne and me kneeling at his feet. I tried to mentally prepare for what was about to occur but couldn't. Instead, a shot of adrenaline flew through me.

Maybe it was the adrenaline, but I couldn't help but think that I was about to bring one of the most powerful men in this country down to his knees.

17

ACE

Having her kneel before me was the hottest thing I'd ever seen. However, watching her take my cock in her mouth would be even better. This would be the perfect way to get her out of my fucking mind.

Her fingers fumbled over my zipper; I assumed nerves were taking over. Before I could make a move to help her, she unbuttoned and unzipped my pants and they fell to my ankles. Being this close to paradise was threatening any shred of patience that I had.

"Am I forcing you to do this?" My words were rough, and I was barely keeping any composure. When she shook her head, I said, "I want to hear you say the words."

I needed to hear her say the words as much as I needed to take my next breath. After having my autonomy stolen in my younger years, I wanted to hear the words fall from her lips.

"I'm not being forced to do this."

"Good. Pull my dick out of my boxer briefs."

Harlow looked up at me before staring at the bulge in my black boxers. As if she'd finally talked herself into it, I watched as she stared at my cock in amazement but didn't move.

"Come on now, Harlow. It's not going to bite."

She hesitated for a moment before taking the head of my cock into her mouth. My eyes shut involuntarily as I took in every sensation she was sending through my body. I forced them back open as she alternated between licking and sucking, moving my erection in and out of her mouth. Watching my dick pass over her red lips was enough to send me over the edge without having her touch me. But having her hand gripping me as she moved her tongue all over me was adding another dimension to the torture she was bringing to my body.

My balls tightened when I heard a small moan come from her mouth, and I gave in to the urge to push my cock gently into her mouth. When she didn't object, I did it again.

The small groan that came from her was almost enough to undo me. I reached over to grip the side of my desk when she took more of me in her mouth. Soon her movements quickened and the mixture of her movements and the sounds that were coming from her mouth made me close my eyes again and force my head to fall back.

We both jumped when the phone rang.

Harlow looked up at me, her eyes wide as the piercing sound of the phone rang around us. I was ready to throw it against the wall.

"Don't stop," I said through gritted teeth. I didn't give a shit if the world was burning down around us. I was going to keep fucking her mouth and then shoot my semen into it.

With clumsy motions, I grabbed my phone and silenced it. If they called back, I wouldn't know it until we were done.

"That's so fucking good." My praise made her moan around me, and that sexy sound combined with the vibration of it around my cock forced a groan from my lips.

I watched her again and I knew I was getting close. I ran my other hand through her blonde hair, enjoying the control that it gave me as her head bobbed up and down on my dick.

"Shit…" I mumbled to myself as my mouth fell open and my release hit me hard. Her swallowing almost every drop deeply satisfied me, and I couldn't wait to sit her ass on my desk, peel away those tight jeans, and feast on her pussy.

Watching a drop of my cum fall out of the side of her mouth before she took her finger and drew it back in was the most erotic thing I'd ever seen. Harlow stood and grabbed a tissue as I was cleaning myself up.

"Next time I'll be coming in that tight pussy of yours. Mark my words."

Those were the words that fell out of my mouth. I smiled to myself when her eyes widened, and a light blush appeared on her cheeks. After what she'd just done, it was amusing to see that my words could have that effect on her.

"Now which car can I use to drive into town?"

My mood did a complete one-eighty. Gone were thoughts of how I could spread her out over my desk. After what had just happened, she was still focused on the car? My mind had jumped to when I could finally make good use of this desk by laying her across it and fucking her into the next decade. "Anderson will give you the keys to one of the cars tomorrow."

I took the tissue out of her hand and gently helped her finish cleaning her face. She stared at my hand before taking a step back.

"What is that on your neck?"

Confusion fell over her face before her hand flew up to cover the area I was referring to on her neck.

"Nothing. I was in a car accident and the seat belt tightened around my neck. I'm fine, really. I put makeup on it to cover it up."

It seemed plausible, but I couldn't help but feel there was more to this story.

Instead of dwelling on it, I decided to shift the conversation back to what had just happened. "I told you I wouldn't do anything that you didn't want to do."

"You told me I had to—"

"I said 'You can get on your knees and put your lips around my cock.' I didn't force you to do either of those actions."

"I wouldn't have gotten your car otherwise."

"Who said that? It was merely a suggestion. Plus, even you said I wasn't forcing you to do anything." I raised an eyebrow at her, daring her to continue this argument.

The blush I'd spotted on her cheeks earlier? It quickly changed to angry blotches. "You are fucking disgusting." I could tell she wanted to say more, but she didn't. Instead, she spun on her heel and stormed out of my office, slamming my door behind her. I adjusted myself and then sat down in my chair. Before I could set off after her and give her an introduction into what I meant by punishments, I checked my phone again and saw who was calling. I growled just before I picked up.

"About time you answered. It's not like you to not take my call on the first go-round. I was about to send someone to check up on you at the 'House on the Hill.'"

I smirked at Gage's nickname for my home. "That's a bit dramatic. I had a matter I was attending to."

"Does this matter have anything to do with the woman that is now living with you? How are things with her by the way?"

"Fine," I said a little too quickly.

Gage snorted. "Things don't sound as if they are going fine."

"Did you just contact me to fuck with me? Or was there another purpose for this call?"

"We actually called about setting up a meeting with all of us. At Elevate? Figured we could meet and let you have free rein of the place in case you wanted to... let off some steam, if you will."

I knew what he was getting at, but I had no intention of taking Harlow there, and I had no intention of fucking anyone else, especially after tonight.

"That should work. I can also see if I can catch another meeting with Falcone while I'm in town. But now it's my turn to ask a favor. Could you or Kingston dig up some information on Harlow? It seems as if you have some time on your hands given how many times you called me tonight when a simple text would have sufficed."

"Fuck you."

I hid the smirk that threatened to take over my face. Even if he couldn't see me, I knew he would be able to tell how I felt based on the sound of my voice. I could have easily done my own search into Harlow and her past, but it was easier to pass it off to Cross Sentinel.

"But I'll dig and see if Kingston or I can find out about her connection to Falcone. And if there are any other red flags, I'll let you know. But be careful. You know she has some connection to Falcone that in itself carries a shit ton of risk and danger."

I could handle Falcone if he tried some shit. "Thanks."

"Don't mention it. We also need to talk about when you'll be back in town for a meeting to debrief Will."

"Okay. And Gage?"

"Yeah, man?"

"All of this could have taken place over email."

"Fuck you," he repeated.

I chuckled before I hung up. There was no way any of this could have been discussed anywhere other than a high secured server if any of this were to be mentioned over email, so the phone call made sense.

As my conversation with Gage faded to the back burner, I let some of my other thoughts consume me.

I couldn't take my mind off her. It was easy to admit it to myself, but I refused to admit it to those I was close to. After all, Kingston had called it and there was no way I was prepared to admit that he had been right.

Thankfully, it hadn't crossed over into any of my business affairs because I couldn't let that happen. Lives could be at stake, and one wrong move could be detrimental to any work I'd been doing up until now. This was going to be a problem.

18

HARLOW

Having the wind flow through my hair like this was what dreams were made of. I don't think I ever felt this carefree in my entire life. Never would I have thought that I would have the opportunity to drive a BMW.

At first, I was nervous about having this much horse-power under my fingertips, but being able to leave on my own terms, even for a short period of time, felt life-changing. I didn't feel as if I was stuck in a prison, at least for the time being.

I'd agreed to return in about an hour and a half.

Ace's home was located about twenty-five minutes outside of Brentson, a college town and home to Brentson University. I'd heard of the town from an acquaintance I'd met about a year or two ago. As I glanced around, I could see why she'd described it as charming, and it was easy to see how people could fall in love with this place and settle down here. It seemed to be a complete one-eighty from the fast-paced life that you'd live in New York City. While my life in NYC didn't allow for much downtime, it allowed me to bury any thoughts or feelings I had about what I had gone through.

Before I could dwell any longer, I found a parking spot and scrambled out of the car. I double-checked that I locked the car three times and said a small prayer that I wouldn't come back to an empty parking spot. Maybe that was a silly mentality to have, but this car wasn't mine. Even if Ace could easily afford to replace it, there was no way I wanted to tack on a stolen vehicle to the tab that I already owed him. I quickly walked across the street and stood in front of Beyond the Page, a cute coffee and bookshop. This had been one of the motivators for me to get out of the house and drive into town. Thoughts of Mama Robinson briefly appeared before I swept them away.

When I pushed open the front door, a gentle bell rang.

"Welcome to Beyond the Page! I'm Chanel, the owner. If you need anything, please just let me know."

I smiled at the woman behind the front desk. "Thank you," I replied softly before turning down the first aisle of books.

I took my time walking up and down the aisle, taking in all the bookstore had to offer and the newfound freedom I had, even though it was temporary. My fingers skimmed the titles of the books on the shelves, and soon I found myself lost in what I considered my personal heaven.

Given that I didn't have to pay for anything since I now lived with Ace, I could treat myself to some new books, since some of mine were still in my studio apartment.

I walked to the back of the bookstore and bought myself a small coffee and took my soon-to-be purchases to the cafe. I cracked open one of the books and quickly got lost in the world that the author created.

"HARLOW."

I jumped and almost flung the book out of my hand. I turned and found Mr. Tall, Dark, and Broody glowering over me.

"Ace? What the heck are you doing here? How did you know where I was?"

"Tracker on the car."

"Of course you would." I mumbled a curse under my breath as I put the books in a neat pile. "That still doesn't explain why you're here."

"Anderson will drive the car back and you're riding with me."

It didn't go unnoticed by me that he ignored my question again. "I can drive the car back to your home, Ace."

"No. You can—"

"Stop. I've done nothing wrong. I've followed the rules that you've laid out, so I should be allowed to drive home." Although I was hyper aware that we were in public, I resisted the urge to look around and see if anyone had stopped to watch this scene unfold. I was doing my best to keep my voice quiet, but stern, because I didn't know who might be watching or listening.

Ace didn't say anything for a moment; instead he studied my face as if to pick apart any weakness he could find. "You know what? You're right."

I stared at him in disbelief. He'd admitted to me being right.

"Anderson can take my car, and you and I can drive back together."

"But I—"

"You'll do the driving, but we need to head out right now."

I wasn't looking forward to being alone in an enclosed space with him, but I still called it a win because I was allowed to drive the car back. The journey was about twenty-five minutes; that was too much time to have to spend with him.

With a heavy sigh, I stood up and grabbed my purse. I left the books behind, and seeing the line that was in front of the cash register, I knew I'd made the right decision since we needed to leave in a hurry.

Due to how busy the bookstore was now, I didn't have an opportunity to tell Chanel goodbye, so I hurried out and found a vehicle double-parked in front of the car I'd driven here. I spotted Anderson in the driver's seat and Ace put a hand on the small of my back and led me toward Anderson's car. Ace relayed the plan and Anderson sped off, giving Ace and me the opportunity to get into the BMW.

Ace opened the driver's door, and I was about to argue with him because I thought he was going back on his word. Instead, he gestured for me to step into the car and when I did, he closed the door behind me and walked around the front. My eyes followed him as he walked to the passenger door and a small shiver ran down my spine. Something had to have caused all this ruckus, but what?

After he was seated in the car, I pulled out of the parking spot. Almost immediately, I could feel Ace's stare on me, causing a slight buzzing energy between us. I wished that I could speed up time and get us back to Ace's estate faster so we could go our separate ways.

But there was something I still wanted to know.

"Now will you tell me what all of that back there was about?"

He didn't answer me right away, and I looked at him out of the corner of my eye. It was then I realized how tense he was. As soon as we got farther away from the bookstore, his body language relaxed.

"You know what I can't seem to keep my mind off of?"

I glanced at him before turning my attention back to the road. "I'm perfectly happy not knowing."

He tapped his finger on the passenger side window and said, "Using my tongue to drive you crazy."

His tone was deep, dripping with arousal. Or was that my pussy?

I shifted in the driver's seat and gripped the steering wheel harder, determined to not let him distract me. Being this close to him, especially when he spoke to me like that, was another intrusion that I didn't need.

"I owe you for the moment in my office and I intend to pay up."

My thoughts drifted back to the blow job I'd given him. It had made me horny as well, and I wished he would have taken me right then and there.

That wasn't something I was ever going to admit to him, however.

"I've fantasized about pulling your hair so that I have ample opportunity to suck on the soft skin on your neck. I want to find every spot on your body that makes you tremble, and you'll unravel in my arms."

"Ace, stop."

"What? Is my confession too much for you?"

"No, but I know that you're using this to once again not answer my question. Now why were you at the bookstore?"

The roles had changed slightly. It was now me demanding the answers.

"The car was stopped for too long and I wanted to make sure you were okay. I called you several times, but you didn't pick up."

I glanced at him out of the corner of my eye. I hadn't even bothered to check my phone since arriving in the bookstore and now guilt clouded my thoughts. Was he telling the truth or lying to hide the real reason? He cared about whether I was okay? That wouldn't have been a reason for us to rush out of the bookstore...

I shook my head at myself. My suspicion of him and practically everyone I encountered was well warranted, but it was exhausting. Normally, I didn't have doubts about my gut, but something made me wonder why I immediately jumped to thinking he was lying about this. Since he'd bought me at an auction, that dynamic played a role, but as far as I knew, he hadn't lied to me, yet the question remained.

LATER THAT EVENING, while lying in bed reading a book, I could hear Ace talking to someone. Was the person in the room with him or were they on the phone? I sat up slowly, trying my best not to make much noise so I could hear. From where I was, I still couldn't tell if he was alone.

I whipped the covers from my body and walked over to our connecting door. Thankfully, I had somehow missed the creaky floorboard that I was sure could be heard from Ace's bedroom.

I placed my ear against the door. I shouldn't be eavesdropping, but I didn't feel guilty about it. If it gave me a leg up when it came to dealing with Ace, then I was willing to do it.

"You want me to set up another meeting with Falcone?"

My eyes widened at his response, but when I didn't hear someone reply out loud, I concluded that he was on the phone, but it wasn't on speaker. I wished I had an idea of who was on the other end or why they needed Ace to talk to Falcone again.

Was this the reason why he'd been away several times since I'd arrived at his estate? Did Falcone have anything to do with it? When Falcone had walked in on Ace signing up to pay my debt and then some, it was obvious that they were familiar with one another, but was there more there?

"Okay, I understand. I need to go."

"Shit," I mumbled to myself. When I heard Ace start to end the call, my stomach slammed into my throat. I knew he had no problem walking into this room whenever he wanted, and I wasn't one hundred percent confident that he wouldn't do it now.

I stepped back from the door and did my best to tiptoe to the bed as quickly as possible. When my foot touched the board that squeaked, I whispered a curse to myself but didn't slow down because it would increase the likelihood of getting caught.

Once I was back in bed, I threw the covers over me and picked up my book as I willed my racing heart to calm down. Seconds ticked on like minutes as I waited to see if Ace would enter my room, but after a few minutes, he didn't. I sucked in a deep breath because I could finally breathe.

Having had my evening interrupted, there was no way I was going to be able to go back to reading my book. I placed the free bookmark that I'd gotten from the coffee shop inside my book and set it on my bedside table.

I turned off the lamp next to my bed and snuggled deep into the covers. I was relieved that he didn't enter my room, but a part of me wished he had.

And that was frightening.

19

ACE

Normally, having the water beat down on my body would be a stress reliever. My bathroom and my bedroom were the only rooms in the house that I'd chosen to put in upgrades to because it provided a sanctuary of sorts. I placed my hands against the cool wet tiles and allowed the water to sluice over me.

It was here that I could wash away the mental stench I had from the activities Kiki had forced me to do. I tried to scrub memories of her touch from my mind, but they still haunted me. Sometimes I could still feel her lips on mine. The guilt that I felt from having to do it and being abused by her often fought a war with one another and no matter which side won, the result was catastrophic.

It had taken me years to admit that what she did was abuse and that was when I vowed to get revenge. I was determined to make her pay for what she'd done.

I kept my word. She wouldn't be able to manipulate, blackmail, or hurt anyone else again. Yet, the hole I had in me still hadn't been filled. I was convinced it never would be. No amount of showers could wipe that clean.

When my shower was finished, I turned the showerhead off and used my hands to wipe the water from my face. I stayed in the tub for a moment longer, enjoying the silence that was everywhere but my mind. With a towel around my waist, I exited the bathroom and into my bedroom.

My bedroom was as dark as my soul. I made sure to tell the interior designer I hired to work on this space that I wanted darker colors and woods and she did a great job implementing the vision in my head.

My thoughts soon drifted to another woman who'd stormed into my life unexpectedly: Harlow.

Today hadn't gone as planned. I gave her the ability to go off on her own and I was willing to admit that I fucked up, but I don't regret doing what I did.

Even if I didn't show it at the time, panic circled through my body when I saw the car that Harlow had driven into Brentson had been parked in one place for too long. My world could be dangerous and with her ties to Falcone, I couldn't be sure that he hadn't done something to hurt her.

So I acted and I was willing to admit that the results were less than stellar, but I did what I needed to do when a potential threat landed at my doorstep. And I'd already made a promise to myself to step up my security efforts in case someone did try to strike.

It would be easiest to let her go and numerous reasons why that should be the case. I could easily forget about our arrangement and the money that I spent to free her from Falcone's clutches.

Being involved with me could prove to be dangerous. I

was currently working with the Mafia on an assignment and who knew if that might backfire, but because she was with me, it could put her life in danger.

She was so fucking young. I remembered what it was like to be twenty-three and you seemingly have your whole life in front of you. I was still waiting on what Gage or Kingston could find that I hadn't, but life hadn't been too sweet to her. This could be an opportunity for a new beginning for her.

But selfishly I couldn't. There was a magnetic pull that I had with her that I couldn't let her go. I'd been trying to avoid her as much as possible, to put some distance between us, so I didn't take her hard and fast. The urge to make her beg for mercy and to protect her at all costs was what had caused today's debacle.

I'm going to do something to make up for the spectacle that was created today. And learn to push back on the emotional impulse decisions that seemed to have plagued me recently. It was why I was in the current situation I was in.

And then I would give in to temptation like I should have done when she first arrived.

20

HARLOW

When I finished washing my face and throwing my hair up into a ponytail, I couldn't help but think of the events that occurred yesterday. Even though it was the next day, there were still so many questions I had about it, but I knew the likelihood of them being answered were slim. Ace kept his thoughts under lock and key from me. Would it be worth trying to pry the answers from him? I wondered about that as I walked out of my bedroom. I almost tripped over a cotton tote bag that had been left near my door, it took me a second to steady myself. I bent down to look inside of it and gasped.

The books that I'd wanted to purchase were sitting in front of me. Ace had bought me the books I was looking at yesterday. How thoughtful was it that he'd made sure that I'd gotten them anyway? I pulled my phone out of my back pocket and texted Ace.

Me: *Are you here?*

Ace: *Yes... missed me?*

I rolled my eyes.

Me: *Where are you?*

Ace: *In my office.*

I thought back to the last time I was in his office and the blow job I'd given him. The memory sent a thunderbolt of desire through my body that was nowhere near as electrifying as the man himself. Instead of being worried about when he was going to claim me, I began to wonder why he hadn't done so already.

I couldn't figure out how I felt about our situation and this present further complicated things.

I grabbed the books and walked down to Ace's office. I knocked once before opening the door and closing it behind me.

"I should be impressed that you at least knocked this time."

"I'm obviously trying here."

Ace turned to look at me, his heated stare burning a hole in me. "Or my threat about punishments is finally starting to sink in."

The way he looked at me made me feel more brazen. "I think that's you voicing your wildest fantasies."

"And soon-to-be reality. I can't wait to stick two fingers into your pussy and drive you to the brink only to stop moving so you can't reach climax, leaving you in agony. And I'll do it again, and again, and again, Sweetness."

For someone who supposedly was horrible at small talk, he had no problem with talking dirty. I had to admit it turned me on when he spoke like that. It was something that I'd never thought would warm me up sexually toward him. Or hell, he'd lit a fire in my body that I'd never experienced before. Sucking his dick and watching him unfold right before my eyes had shifted my thoughts from being worried about what he might do in the bedroom to being intrigued.

"You bought me these books."

He stood up and said, "I did."

"Uh, thank you."

"You're welcome. Marnie mentioned how bored you've been living here, and I wanted to make sure that you had something to keep you occupied."

Interesting that he'd asked Marnie about me.

"There's something else."

He didn't say a word as he pushed the black velvet box toward me. I found my breath again when I realized it wasn't a square box, but rectangular.

"What is this?"

He didn't respond to me with words, instead warming me with his dark gaze, daring me to open the box. When I did, my eyes widened, and I looked up at him. There was a sleek gold bracelet with diamonds all over it inside. If I had to guess, it had to have cost thousands of dollars.

"It's stunning. What's this for?"

"Just a gift."

"But why?" I couldn't remember the last time someone had gifted me something. I took the bracelet out and stared at it in amazement.

"I saw it and it made me think of you."

"Books and a bracelet... all in one day."

"I went into the bookstore to pick up the books and the jewelry shop was next door."

I remembered seeing the store when I walked into the bookstore but didn't pay much attention to it. Apparently, Ace had. "You bought it yourself?"

He nodded. "Do you see any assistants here? I have several that work for my business entities, but none of them are here."

His explanation still left me shocked. Ace picked the bracelet out himself and that fascinated me. The books were a thoughtful gift and made sense because of where he'd found me in town the day he'd freaked out. He bought me a piece of jewelry just because? I didn't believe that no matter how beautiful it was.

He walked around the desk and came to stand in front of me. He pulled the bracelet out of its resting place and then grabbed my arm to maneuver it where he wanted. His touch seared a mark on me that only I could see and feel.

Now that he seemed more willing to talk, I knew this was my chance to ask more questions. "It seems as if you're very involved with the company. Anderson told me that you've been away on business a couple of times since I arrived."

"You could say that."

That's not suspicious. "What else could I say about it?"

Ace crossed his arms. "It's not something you need to worry about."

"Oh? Does that imply there is something I need to worry about?"

Ace smirked. "You might worry about what I'm going to do to you tonight."

That sent a little thrill through me. "And what might that be?"

"Why spoil the surprise?"

I rolled my eyes as another thought occurred to me. "Ace, why were you at that auction? Are you in the same business as Falcone?"

Ace closed his eyes briefly and I could see that he was losing patience with me. I wondered if he would answer my question. I didn't think the conclusion I'd reached was too far-fetched.

"I'm not in the same business as Falcone, and I'm sure many people received an invitation to the auction."

Before I could ask another question, Ace's phone rang. He stared at me for a moment before he broke eye contact and looked at the screen.

"I need to take this," he said.

I nodded and turned to walk away. Before I could take a step, I felt him grab my hand.

"You'll join me for dinner tonight. You are to wear something from the closet."

He wasn't giving me an opportunity to turn him down. His tone gave a lingering hint of what might lie ahead tonight.

21

ACE

I couldn't help but be pleased that she was speechless about the bracelet. It had taken me more time to select than I wanted to admit, but I thought it would be perfect for her.

I looked down at the screen again and answered the phone. "Yes?"

"I found some information on your girl."

I didn't bother correcting him because I knew he said it to get under my skin. "What is it, Kingston?"

"Gage is on the line too."

"Of course he is. He wouldn't miss this for the world."

"You know it," Gage chimed in.

"That's fine. The information that you found better not be that she was given up when she was born and bounced from foster home to foster home as a child. I knew that already." Staying up late after I'd locked her in her bedroom had been a productive time for me.

"So, you also know about the woman who adopted her when she was a preteen?"

"Yes, I found that out in my own research." I wished that she'd been the one to tell me about her upbringing, but we didn't have that type of relationship.

"We found out that she borrowed a large sum of money from Falcone to pay for her adoptive mother's funeral expenses."

I nodded as I rolled the information around in my head. "That answers one question but creates another."

"What's that?" Gage asked.

"How had she gotten in contact with Falcone in the first place?"

"That we don't know."

After a couple of more minutes on the phone, I wrapped things up with Gage and Kingston. I looked at the clock and saw that the call had delayed me longer than I'd planned. I rose and left my office to meet Harlow for dinner.

My insistence on having dinner with her whenever I was home had a purpose. Sharing a meal with someone was something I didn't get a chance to do nearly enough, and this gave me the perfect opportunity to do so.

When I walked into the dining room, Harlow was already seated, and Marnie had just set some food down in front of her.

I thanked Marnie before she left, and Harlow and I began to eat. I found myself staring at her as she sat across from me during dinner. Once again, Marnie had created chicken Kiev and I knew that it would be a delicious meal that both of us were eager to enjoy.

It pleased me that she'd worn the dress I'd asked her to wear the last time we had dinner together. That, paired with the bracelet that I'd given her, made me want to lift her onto this table and fuck her until we both were seeing double.

But I couldn't, at least not tonight, because I was leaving within the hour.

"I'm heading into the city for a business meeting, but I should be back before morning."

"Happy to see you again, Mr. Bolton."

"Likewise, Mr. Falcone." It was easy to lie and make it seem as if we both wanted to be in the same room as one another when we didn't.

I'd met with Falcone in his office in the basement of Bar 53 again.

"To what do I owe this meeting? Is everything okay with Harlow?"

Interesting that the first thing he thought was that something must have happened between Harlow and me to cause me to call him. "I wanted to discuss more of the business opportunities that you had in mind. Everything with Harlow is perfect. She's kept up her end of the deal nicely."

That led to a wicked smile appearing on his face. "I knew she'd be perfect. She ended up being a last-minute addition to the event, and boy, am I glad I had the bright idea of putting that together. I knew that she'd be something."

This conversation was starting to become interesting, but I kept my expression neutral. "What gave you the idea that she'd be 'something'?"

"I didn't expect to spend this much time talking about her."

His response was strange. I shrugged but kept my expression blank, making sure not to let him know that I was feeding for more information about Harlow. "Neither did I, but I'm curious to hear your expert opinion."

While my voice sounded more sarcastic with every word, Falcone didn't pick up on any of it. "My right-hand man, Ian, had a small taste of her so I knew that adding her to the lineup of the auction was the right idea. And I was right as shown by how pleased you are."

Ian had a taste of her? "And your wallet is a million dollars fatter, so I'm not the only one who was pleased."

Falcone nodded. "That I can't complain about."

"Did she and Ian date before or something?"

Falcone waved his hand. "No, but I had to separate them from one another at Bar 53 because an incident occurred between the two of them, but it was resolved."

"It doesn't sound like it was resolved, Falcone."

Falcone tapped the side of his head with his index finger. "It is because she's all yours now. Before we waste any more time, what business dealings did you want to discuss?"

I watched his eyes follow me, studying me closely, probably trying to figure out if he could trust me or not. He looked down at some of the papers on his desk before looking back up at me.

"I'm curious to know if the auction the other night is the only business dealings you are involved in." I knew it wasn't but if this would get him to admit what he was doing and where he was doing it.

"We do auctions on a much larger scale..."

The conversation continued with me pivoting whenever he tried to make me give him an answer about what my involvement might be, but he refused to give any more information about what else he was involved in or where he was doing business out of, but I felt as if I was getting closer. As I stood up to shake his hand at the end of our meeting, I had one more question that I had to ask.

"What business did you have with my grandfather?"

"I was wondering when you would ask that."

I saved it for last for this very reason. I'd gone back through the files, both paper and electronic, that I still had from his tenure and asked Anderson if my grandfather had mentioned anything to him but turned up with nothing.

"We can save that for another time."

I wanted to push him on it, but I needed to think of the bigger picture that had just become enormous. I needed to be careful because of the information I was trying to dig up for Will and now what he'd hinted at about Harlow and Ian.

This time, Falcone himself, along with the guard who was watching his office door, escorted me to the entrance of Bar 53, where my driver for the evening was waiting. As I sat in the backseat of the car, my mind tried to process what I'd learned from what he said and was ready to take it back to Kingston and Will, my mind was still partially on what he'd announced about Harlow.

What was he protecting Ian from? If I couldn't get Falcone to say more or Harlow to admit to me what had happened, I had no problem going to visit Ian myself.

22

HARLOW

As I walked down the stairs, the front door opened and Ace walked in, looking as if he'd just stepped off the front cover of a fashion magazine. His dark suit and tie fit him impeccably and I felt underdressed in my jeans, T-shirt, and flats. It still felt weird having access to that closet with all of those clothes that cost more than I might ever make in my lifetime.

When I reached the landing, he gestured for me to walk in front of him and I followed suit. His hand briefly fell to the small of my back and the pressure from its presence heightened my awareness of how close I was to him. After I sat down, he pushed my chair in just as Marnie appeared with our dinner that smelled amazing as usual. She placed the dishes in front of us and poured each one of us a glass of Pinot Noir.

Marnie didn't linger around and exited the room wrapping up her duties. I studied the meal, debating whether it was worth asking the question and risk feeling embarrassed about it. But I wouldn't know until I did it...

"Ace?"

He didn't answer verbally, choosing to dip his head once, encouraging me to go ahead.

"What type of meat is this?"

"Duck breast."

So it was duck breast with some kind of sauce. Embarrassment didn't crawl to the surface and make itself known on my face. I'd never had duck before, so it wasn't too surprising that I had no idea what it was. I stabbed the meat with my fork and placed it in my mouth. The flavors from the duck and the sauce melted in my mouth and I couldn't help but sigh happily at the sensations my mouth was experiencing.

After a few moments of enjoying the food that seemed to be hitting all of the right places on my taste buds, I asked, "Was everything okay?"

"What do you mean?"

I remained fixated on the food in front of me. "You just came back from the city, and I was curious about why you went there for business on a Sunday. You travel back and forth an awful lot."

"I have businesses to run, Harlow."

He stated it as if it was the most reasonable explanation in the entire world. It did make sense, but didn't most people take the weekend off? Should I chalk it up to him being a workaholic?

"Tell me about Ian."

That got my attention. "What about him? He's just a former coworker."

Ace leaned forward, becoming more intimidating. "Falcone seemed to allude that there was more to it than that."

"Why were you meeting with him to begin with?"

"Business, Harlow."

"You don't have to use that tone with me. It was a simple question since that seems to be what we are doing right now. Asking simple questions."

Ace sighed and ran a hand through his short brown locks. "It was a business meeting about ways we might be able to collaborate in the future. Now tell me about Ian. Falcone alluded to it being the reason that you ended up being a part of his auction."

I found myself staring down at my plate again wondering how I should answer this. Although Ace had no obligation to do so, he could have told me he was going to see Falcone, and would he believe me if I told him what Ian really did to me? I quickly made a decision.

"Ian and I have been working at Bar 53 together for months... or hell, has it been a year? Anyway, he and I have never really gotten along. Things spilled over into us working together and of course Falcone picked Ian. And now here I am." I gestured to myself.

I looked up and found Ace's gaze on me. He didn't say anything as he studied me, I assume trying to decipher whether I was lying or not. I kept my facial expression blank as I stared back at him, determined not to show any reason for him not to believe the words that had just fallen from my lips.

He took a sip from the wine Marnie served us before pushing his chair back. When he stood up, my eyes followed him, and a sinking feeling lodged itself in my stomach.

"Stand up," he said.

I bought myself some time by wiping my lips as his long

stride ate up the distance between us. My breath caught in my throat as I too pushed back my chair and stood up. He grabbed my hand for a split second and led me to another portion of the table before turning me around so that I was facing him again. He enclosed my body with his and just before my ass could touch the dining room table, he lifted me up, forcing me to sit on the surface.

"Eating dinner wasn't the only thing I had in mind."

His eyes stared at my lips for a moment, and I wondered if he might kiss them. I was slightly disappointed when he spoke again. "Lean back on your elbows."

"But the dishes—"

"Are not in your way. Do as I say."

I hesitated for a moment before I looked over my shoulder to confirm that, in fact, my body wouldn't hit anything. The hardness of the table underneath my body and his stare felt as if he was looking through me. The thought was unnerving because I could see him reading me, forming his opinions about what he thought he knew about me. Why I was starting to care what he thought was beyond me.

"Good girl."

Those simple words made me want to melt into a puddle on this table. What was coming over me?

I watched as he removed my flats. Then he dragged two fingers up my leg, leaving a trail of goose bumps and nerves in his wake. His hands came together when his fingers reached the top button of my jeans. He stared into my eyes as he unbuttoned them, daring me to tell him no. Even though I was nervous, there was not a chance in hell that I was going to do that.

He didn't break eye contact as he slowly slid my zipper down. "Lift up your hips."

"But what about Marnie or Anderson walking in?"

"Don't worry about them, they won't."

His reassurance did little to remove the question from my mind. Once again, I found myself following his orders and slowly he peeled my jeans away. I swallowed hard as he broke eye contact with me and studied my half-unclothed body. My underwear was nothing special, but it didn't seem to matter to him.

His hands took up the mantle once more as he moved my panties to the side so that he could see my pussy.

"So pretty," he mumbled, more to himself than to me as he dragged his finger up and down my slit. The soft touch caused butterflies to grow in my stomach. I watched him as if trapped under a spell that he'd cast.

He watched me as he bent down between my open legs, and I couldn't look away. His eyes closed as he began to feast on my pussy. I sighed when his lips touched mine, but my body tensed up and it was clear that he'd noticed. He stopped moving and pulled back before looking up at me.

"What's wrong?"

A look of puzzlement crossed his face. "Are you a virgin?"

"No. I've never had someone... do that before."

"Lick your pussy?"

"Yes." My lips snapped shut, suddenly fear of what his reaction might be.

"That's a travesty because you deserve this pleasure, Sweetness. But now I'm going to make sure that you get it and more."

I could care less about the silly nickname he'd given me if

he kept looking at me like that. With more determination in his eyes, he shifted my body so that I sat near the edge of the table. He put his hands on my thighs, effectively anchoring me in place and leaned back toward my pussy.

My whole world ceased to exist from there.

Ace alternated between licking and sucking me. It was as if the food we'd just eaten was the appetizer and I was the main course. My thighs trembled before I could stop them, and a loud groan fell from my lips.

"That's my girl," I heard him mumble against me, but I couldn't give a shit about what he referred to me as right now.

The noises that were coming out of my mouth seemed to serve as his motivation because he sped up and I couldn't stop my head from falling back. My body had a mind of its own as my hips rocked against his face, trying to get as close as possible to him.

What I hadn't realized was that he moved one of his hands that had been resting on my thighs and slid a finger inside of me.

"Oh my fucking—"

The words were lost as Ace was doing everything to drive me mad. If he stopped now, I would cry.

"You're close."

Him telling me what I was would have normally pissed me off, but I didn't care, and he was right.

"Come for me, baby,"

The harshness of my breath was music to my own ears. I closed my eyes as my body careened out of control. Finding my release was a blessing, but I was afraid of what I might see when I opened them.

Once I gained control of my bearings, I slowly lifted my

eyelids and caught his stare and noticed the hunger in his eyes, the need to continue to devour me was blaring in them like a siren. But it was as if a light switch had flickered. He took a step back to admire his handiwork, a smirk appeared on his face.

"You taste just like I thought you would." He stuck his fingers in his mouth. The motion I was sure would lead me to come all over again. "You should clean up before Marnie or Anderson comes in here to collect the dishes."

He gave me one last glance before he left the room, leaving me staring behind him.

23

HARLOW

few afternoons later, I eased myself into the pool. I thought the water would be more shocking to my system, but it was relatively warm. I closed my eyes and rested my arms on the edge of the pool, taking in the way the water swayed around my body.

When my body had grown used to being in the water I started swimming, enjoying the way my body moved through the pool. A couple of years ago I had gotten a membership to a local gym, and someone had offered to give me swimming lessons for free, but the first few times that I had gotten into the water had been terrifying. Over time I learned how to cruise through the water. I was by no means an Olympic-level swimmer but learning how to swim had eventually become a great stress reliever. And in my opinion, it was an important skill to have. I did several laps through the pool before I came to a stop.

I stood up in the water and ran my hands across my eyes. For some reason, I wasn't surprised to find Ace staring back at me. Thankfully, by the time I decided to try out his pool, the bruises faded enough that it was hard to notice that they'd been there at all so no makeup was necessary. Having to explain them was the last thing I wanted to do. "You were watching me."

"I was. Didn't know you could swim."

"There's still a lot you don't know about me."

"Yet there's plenty you know about me... intimately."

I rubbed my hand across my face again, trying to mask the heat that was rising on my neck and would eventually make its way up to my cheeks.

"Is there something you wanted?" I didn't wait for him to respond before I took a couple of strokes as I swam toward the stairs. I wrung out my hair as I stepped out of the pool before adjusting the one-piece suit that I found in one of the drawers in my room.

I turned to face him and found him staring at me. He didn't try to avert his eyes even when he knew I'd caught him. His eyes landed on my breasts, leaving me breathless and forgetting to grab my towel that I'd left on a chair near the pool. Given the chill in the air, I could assume that my nipples were standing at attention. His eyes lowered down toward my legs before making their way back up my curves. It was me who snapped out of it first and quickly grabbed the towel and wrapped it around my body. I'd been chilly when I exited the pool, but when I noticed him staring at me, I could feel my temperature rising.

When he continued to look at me instead of responding, I said, "You haven't answered my question."

"To see you. Anderson mentioned that you were swimming in the pool."

He came down to see me for no reason? Didn't he have anything more important to do?

I slipped my flip-flops on and said, "Okay. Well, I'm going to go take a shower to get this chlorine off so I'll see you later."

I half expected him to grab me as I walked past him, but he didn't say or do anything as I made my way out of the pool area and up to my room. Quickly closing my bedroom door behind me, I walked into the bathroom and turned on the shower. While the water heated up, I took off the towel and my swimsuit and once the water was at a temperature I could tolerate, I slipped into the shower.

As I lathered my body in soap, I relived my encounter with Ace at the pool. The way that his eyes studied me was unnerving yet enthralling. Under his gaze, I felt scared and alive at the same time. The contradiction that I felt within myself was problematic.

I walked back into my bedroom with a towel on and gasped when I found Ace sitting on my bed. His eyes slowly made their way up my body before they landed on my face. I found the look in his eyes troubling. I licked my lips, wishing that I could hold my hands close together, but that meant that I would risk exposing my naked body to him.

But that seemed to have been the same thing he was thinking, because he said, "Drop the towel."

I didn't move, but I could sense the shift in the temperature. Him being in the room, sitting on the edge of my bed and demanding that I remove the last shred of my dignity. I had no words to express how I was feeling, although I had been expecting this to happen eventually. After all, this was the reason I was here.

"I've been trying to avoid touching you for a long time and I've failed twice. Now, I won't be denied anymore. I paid—"

That snapped me out of my speechlessness. "Can you stop reminding me of that? Even just for a moment?"

"All right." He stood up and said, "Do you want me to whisper sweet nothings in your ear? Try to make this more romantic? You didn't strike me as someone who wanted romance."

"You don't know anything about me."

"I know more than you think, Sweetness."

In response, I dropped the towel defiantly and with more confidence than I possessed. His jaw stiffened and he strolled over to me as if he didn't have anything else to be concerned about but me. I felt my breasts tighten with every step he took, knowing that he was going to stake his claim over my body.

He took his time studying me, as if I was the only thing that mattered in his world. He shifted his body weight, making himself appear larger than life, and said, "What I do know is that you're never going to be the same after this."

Before I could ask what he meant, he was on me. I was done trying to fight the connection I knew we shared. I turned my face slightly to give him a chance to catch my lips with his, but he avoided my attempt.

The slight dejection I felt fell away when he pulled me even closer to him, my breasts meeting the fabric of his shirt. Where I expected him to be smoother in his movements, he was erratic, as if every moment his hands weren't on me was time wasted.

He wanted this as much as I did.

Ace lifted me up with ease, laid me down on the bed, and stared at me once again from head to toe. My nipples tingled in anticipation as he stared at them, as if completely enthralled. Gone were the thoughts of how I couldn't trust him, and in their place were desire and the need to have his body on mine.

He moved so that he was leaning over me and I sighed when he lightly sucked on my nipple. *Finally.*

Giving in to this pull he had on me was one of the best decisions I'd made. When he sucked harder, I moaned. I couldn't believe how much I was ready to throw everything away just because he was driving me wild by sucking my nipple.

Ace switched breasts and after a few licks, he lightly bit down.

"Making sure that you're paying attention," he mumbled against my breast before he went back to sucking on my nipple. As if I could be paying attention to anything else.

I tried to appear confident in everything that I did. Nothing about having sex with Ace was faked as another shot of desire filled me.

While his mouth was focused on my nipples, his fingers had a mind of their own. They were on a journey down my body, and they didn't stop until they reached my pussy. When his fingertips found my clit, I shuddered due to how sensitive I was, but that didn't stop him. I cried out when his fingers slipped between my walls.

"Someone is enjoying this immensely," Ace said, but it sounded as if he was far away instead of right over me. He removed his lips from my breasts and turned all of his focus to giving my pussy the attention it craved.

The pressure within me began to build. He slid down and added his mouth to the chaos he was putting me through. I could feel my body giving way to the pleasure he was creating within me.

"I—I—" I couldn't find the words as my pussy pulsated around his fingers and brought me the release I'd been longing for.

"Delicious," he said as he continued to lick me and helped me ride out the orgasm that had just rocked my life. He removed himself from me and I was left still questioning if my soul had left my body or not.

My pussy ached for him when he stood up and took a step back.

"You don't know how beautiful you look at this very moment," Ace said as his stare followed my every movement while he undressed himself.

I too found myself staring at his cock once more. Without waiting another second, he lined his cock up with my entrance and sank into me.

"Fuck, baby."

I trembled at the sound of his voice. He could say whatever he wanted as long as he kept thrusting his cock into me. Ace stared at where we were joined together for a moment before his eyes gravitated toward mine. The dark orbs contained so many emotions in them, but I had no idea what they meant. What I did know was at this very point, as far as he and I were concerned, this right here was perfect.

"You don't know how good this feels." The words rushed out of my mouth.

"I think I have a fairly good idea," Ace replied as his tempo picked up.

I hadn't been expecting it to feel even better. He continued thrusting himself in and out of me until we both went careening over the edge, our orgasms leaving us both breathless.

When he shifted his body, I groaned before I froze. It was then I realized that I hadn't heard the distinct sound of a wrapper being opened. Had he used a condom?

When he removed himself from me, I got the answer I wanted and dreaded. We'd both forgotten.

I could see on his face when he too realized that we hadn't used one, as he walked into the bathroom stark naked. I wondered what he was going to do next. Would he get back into bed? But he got dressed, with the precision of someone who hadn't just been fucked. I wasn't all that surprised that he didn't want to cuddle, but the rejection was still there. Here he'd rocked my world completely and he wanted to get away from me as quickly as possible. We also hadn't addressed the elephant in the room.

I followed his lead and picked up the towel he'd told me to drop. I debated whether I wanted to put on the clothes that I had set out on the dresser, but I nixed that idea in favor of another shower.

"I'll see you at dinner."

Flashes of what we'd just done and what happened the evening before flew through my mind as he left the room, in much the same fashion that he'd done after dinner the evening before. I was left longing for the connection we'd just shared. This was what he meant by coming to collect.

24

ACE

Deep down, I knew I was fucked. Not only had fucking her not doused any of the desire that I felt for her, but I'd had sex with her without a condom. Never in the years that I'd been having sex had I forgotten to use one. The first time with her, I screwed up.

I wanted her again and again, to the point where I was even tempted to walk through the door connecting our rooms and take her again. After all, that was the reason I'd put her in the room next to mine.

This wasn't supposed to be the case. I'd hoped that finally sinking my cock into her warm cunt would have affected the desire that I had for her.

But it hadn't.

What had changed was the promise I made to myself about keeping Harlow. At least there were still over two months left in our contract where I could take her any which way possible before it was time to set her free.

Because she shouldn't be here with me.

THIRTY MINUTES BEFORE DINNER, I found Harlow sitting in my living room reading another book, confirming that my purchase from the bookstore was a good one. I also noticed that she'd put on a nicer shirt since I'd left her naked in her bedroom. I was willing to bet it was one of the pieces I'd ordered from a fancy boutique in the city. The amount I paid for them to ship the clothes as soon as possible had been well worth it based on how good the clothes looked on her and how much I wanted them to end up on the floor of her bedroom.

She was so lost in the book, she didn't notice me staring at her, drinking her all in undisturbed.

I cleared my throat and Harlow looked up.

"We need to talk."

"Oh?" she said and sat up.

"Yes. We didn't use a condom."

"I knew after I had to clean the mess that was left."

I cursed myself for not thinking to stay and help clean her up. I'd been so focused on getting the hell out of dodge that nothing else had mattered.

"Did you come in here to gloat?"

Her question took me off guard. "No, I came in here to confirm your health status."

She scoffed. "Sounds like something we should have discussed before you stuck your dick in me, doesn't it? Hell, even before I gave you a blow job."

It was clear that we had a history of not taking the proper precautions before it came to being intimate, but I was going to rectify that right now.

"I'm clean. Got tested a month ago and haven't had sex with anyone besides you since then."

"And I'm clean too. Haven't had sex with anyone in months. I'm also on birth control, so the chances of a pregnancy are almost nonexistent."

Hearing that she was on birth control was a relief, and I was happy that we didn't have to use condoms. If she hadn't been on birth control, we would have dealt with the consequences as they arose, and I would have done everything I could to ensure that both of us would have remained safe without using a condom. After having a taste of her without a barrier between us, there was no way I would willingly switch to using one.

I briefly wondered what she would look like heavily pregnant with my child. Just as quickly as the thought entered my mind, I swiftly pushed it to the side because she wasn't staying here.

"Now that we've gotten that out of the way, I want to take you on a tour of the property. Anderson gave you a tour of the house, but I want to take you around the rest of it. We need to drive because walking would take too long."

She raised an eyebrow before standing up and stretching her arms. The motion lifted her shirt, causing me to see a sliver of her belly. I felt my dick harden at the sight, further confirming how fucked I was. Just seeing a touch of her skin had caused that.

"Let me grab something to put over my arms and I'll be ready to go."

I grabbed her arm before she could walk away. "Wait, there is something I wanted to give you."

I pulled the item out of my pocket and handed it to her.

"A credit card?"

"Whatever you need while staying here that we might not have, feel free to charge it to the card."

Harlow looked at the card, then back at me. "Thank you."

"You're welcome."

She hesitated for a moment before she grabbed her things and walked out of the living room. I was left behind, staring at the empty space she'd left.

I gathered what I needed for our short excursion and found Harlow chit-chatting with Marnie and Anderson near the front door. I'd assumed that the two might be interacting with Harlow especially when I wasn't here, but it was interesting to see it in action. When the group heard me approach, Marnie gave us both a small wave and exited the hallway, while Anderson opened the front door for us. Soon we were riding in my BMW, this time with me at the wheel.

"This property is... interesting."

I looked at Harlow before I turned my attention back to the road in front of us. "Are you referring to the run-down nature of it all?"

"I guess I wasn't subtle about that at all."

"Not one bit."

She laughed before she said, "Neither the interior nor the exterior fit someone who is closer to my age than Anderson's."

"How do you know I'm closer to your age than Anderson's?"

"There's no way you're over the age of like twenty-nine even with the little gray coming into your scruff."

"Thirty-seven."

The shock that registered on her face when I admitted my

age was comical. I wasn't surprised about our fourteen-year age gap given the information I knew about her. Still, Harlow had a good point.

"You're right. My grandfather sold the property to me and for the most part, I don't pay attention to what the inside of the house looks like."

"Because you're traveling back and forth to the city quite a bit."

"Right." I didn't elaborate because it didn't make any sense in involving her in the intricacies of the businesses that I'd inherited. Some of them were legal, while others were illegal much like my investigation into what shit Falcone was getting into. Plus, the purpose of this drive was to give us some time away from the house and for me to find out more about her, but it seemed as if once again, she'd turned the tables on me.

"Do you feel comfortable here?"

I tossed her question around in my mind, trying to figure out an answer that was truthful but didn't give too much away. "It's complicated."

"I think if you took the time to make this place your own, you'd be happier."

"Or I could just sell it."

I saw Harlow nod out of the corner of my eye. "That is another option, but I get the feeling that you wouldn't want to do that."

And how right she was. Selling the property and reaping the profits would be a nice benefit, but something about this property kept me chained to it.

Maybe it was the fact that my grandfather was still alive that made me hesitant to sell it even though the property was in my name. Sure, my relationship with my grandfather wasn't the greatest throughout my life, but keeping this in the family, at least for now, seemed like the best option. Changing a few things in the home wouldn't be the worst thing in the world.

"Do you have any ideas of what should be changed?"

My question seemed to surprise Harlow, who stared at me for a moment before responding. "You know that you could easily hire designers whose job it is to do this type of thing, right? This isn't my forte."

"So? I'm asking you. What would you change?"

I genuinely wanted to know how she felt about my home.

"Let me start with that. I absolutely love the library. It can stay exactly as it is."

"I'm not surprised you feel that way."

"I also love the pool."

"I love that you love the pool."

She tapped my hand with one of hers and grinned. "Can you ever not think about sex?"

I shrugged. It was hard to not think about having sex with her whenever she was near. "What else would you change?"

"Some of the wallpaper has to go. It's too much and dates the house tremendously. It also makes the home feel dark and creepy. Also, for the love of everything, updating the kitchen for Marnie alone would do wonders for everyone."

"Duly noted."

The teasing smile she sent me made me feel something that was rare for me to feel: happy.

25

HARLOW

The hold he had over me was indescribable. It was several days after we'd taken the trip around his property and every evening after that, he'd snuck into my room through the connecting door and came to my bed.

This was a bad idea, yet I craved him more than my next breath.

He whipped my nightgown over my head and flipped me over. He massaged my ass before his hand landed on it with a decisive slap. He'd discovered several days ago how much I loved having him play with my ass and took every opportunity to do so.

"That's for prancing around in that bathing suit when you knew damn well what it would do to me."

"No one told you to continue coming down to watch me while I swam alone."

He slapped my ass again and I moaned. He was bringing my cravings to new heights. He pulled my lower body up so that I was on all fours and slid his cock into me without another thought.

Ace pounded into me again and I sighed. He leaned over and grabbed my hair lightly but firmly as he continued to move his body with mine. It was obvious that this would be a quick one, and I was perfectly okay with that.

When his hand reached around our bodies and found my clit, I almost fell face-first into the pillow underneath me. Our bodies moved together to speed things up and I swore I'd bitten my lip so hard I was convinced that I'd drawn blood.

"Stop holding back, Harlow."

"Fuck... Ace!" I screamed, not caring who in the home heard. This was steadily developing into a habit for the both of us.

This wasn't like anything I'd done before, and I got the feeling that I wouldn't experience this kind of thing with anyone else ever again.

"Let go, Harlow."

His encouragement sent my body over the edge, spiraling into the abyss that only he could send me into. He pulled me up so that his chest was smashed up against my back and continued moving, allowing me to ride out my climax. His grunt was the only thing that warned me that he was about to come, and when the low groan left his mouth it was music to my ears.

When his body left mine, this time I snatched my night-gown off the bed and walked into the bathroom to clean myself. I did it without a word, because if the nightly ritual of us fucking was a hint, he'd soon get dressed and leave me there without another word.

I'd tried to tell myself that him choosing to leave after sex didn't hurt, but it did. I pushed the thoughts from my mind while we were together so I could enjoy the moment, but soon I'd be alone again, left to my own thoughts that had no problem torturing my soul.

When I double-checked that I looked presentable again, I opened the door and found him sitting on the edge of my bed, buttoning up his shirt and I assumed about to pull the disappearing act that he was well versed in. It was interesting how none of our talks that we had during the day has translated into anything else in the bedroom outside of the dirty talk we shared while having sex.

He rose from the bed and looked at me, his expression unreadable as he took me all in. It was as if we'd gone from being intimate with one another, where we both knew each other's wants and needs, to being complete strangers once more.

What I'd gotten myself into with Ace was more dangerous than anything I'd been involved in my entire life. Moving in and out of people's lives was easy when no one really expected you to stay, but somehow, I wished that there was a deeper connection for us even though in the end, I more than likely would be the one who ended up hurt.

And it didn't go unnoticed that he still hadn't kissed me.

I COULDN'T HELP but smile as I stepped out of the car. Getting out of the house felt wonderful and being back in this charming small town was well worth the drive. I locked the car door behind me and walked the few feet to the entrance and heard a familiar chime when I entered.

"Harlow! Lovely to see you again."

I stood back and blinked at the woman, slightly confused by her comment because I didn't remember giving her my name. "How did you know my name?"

Being recognized felt weird. I was used to fading into the background, not being seen or heard unless someone tried to start shit with me. This felt strange but normal.

"Oh shoot." She closed her eyes and shook her head at herself. "Ace Bolton mentioned it when he came back to grab the books you left behind. How have you been? It's been a couple of weeks or so since you were last here?"

"Good, good." It wasn't a lie. I'd been doing well. Ace and I weren't trading snappy remarks nearly as much, and when we did, they were more playful in nature. Still, I longed for something deeper between us, but that was neither here nor there.

I'd decided to go back to Beyond the Page to pick up a few more books including a couple of new releases that I'd had my eye on. This was a reasonable thing to use the credit card that Ace had given me on.

I smiled at Chanel and walked over to the new releases table. I picked up the two books that I wanted and wandered down the aisles to see if any other books caught my eye.

Seeing nothing else, I headed to the front desk so that Chanel could ring me up.

"You're going to love this book. I just know it. Did you enjoy the books that you got last time?"

I nodded. "I blew through them quickly, which is a blessing and a curse."

"Yes, I told Ace that it might make sense for him to add a few more to the pile of books that he was buying for you because you seemed like the type of person who had no problem finishing books within a day, let alone a week."

Chanel and Ace having a conversation about me, and my book habit was endearing in a way. He could have easily sent Anderson to pay for the books, but he came back here himself and bought them along with the bracelet. Him running errands on my behalf brought me joy for a split second before I tamped it down.

He'd already said that all our relationship would ever be was sex, so I needed to lower my expectations, because all it would do is lead to a whole lot of hurt.

26

HARLOW

Three days later, I walked into Ace's kitchen because the scents coming from it were heavenly. I found Marnie standing over a pot, stirring with a wooden spoon.

"Marnie?" I asked, trying not to startle her. I failed.

"Oh!" she said as she spun around and looked at me. "Harlow, you scared me."

"I'm sorry." I gave her a smile. When she returned it, my heart swelled slightly. The warmth in her eyes was rare for me to see, let alone have directed at me. Between her and Anderson, they were the nicest people I'd ever met, and it was hard not to wonder how they got along with Ace, who seemed to be more closed off than the two of them combined.

"What are you up to?" she asked.

"Nothing much. I got distracted when I smelled what you were cooking." I walked over to the kitchen counter and leaned on it.

She looked behind her and smiled again before turning back to the pot. "I told Mr. Bolton that keeping you locked up in that room would get boring quickly, but at least you've gotten the opportunity to go to Brentson. As you've probably already figured out, there's not much to do around here, and I think that is what the elder Bolton wanted."

"Can you tell me about him?" I asked.

Marnie looked at the pot but was silent. I suspected she was wondering whether she should continue with this conversation. With a deep sigh, she said, "Honey, you might want to sit down if we're going to get into what the elder Bolton is like."

My eyebrows shot up for a split second and I took my seat at the counter. There was no way that I was going to miss this conversation in hopes that it might help me piece together some things about Ace.

"Jerald Bolton is a stern man. He took no BS from his family or when it came to his business."

"I wonder if that's where Ace got it from," I mumbled.

"Ace is nothing like that."

I shook my head at myself when I realized I'd spoken my thoughts out loud. I really needed to get better about doing that.

Marnie looked at me before she continued. "There's still some warmth to Mr. Bolton that I think is nowhere to be found in his grandfather. Frankly, I'm glad he left."

"Do you know why Ace's grandfather is so cold?"

"Not sure. What I do know is that there were stories about how he kicked his daughter out when she got pregnant with Ace, and she was only a teen."

That admission stunned me. "He kicked his child out when she probably needed him the most?"

"I'm not sure about his reasons for doing so, but even

though I've been here for twenty years, I'd only met Ace on a number of occasions, and his mother maybe once or twice. I'm not sure if Mr. Bolton and his daughter ever patched up their relationship before she died."

"She died?"

"Yep, she died when Ace was still a child. Mr. Bolton paid for her funeral, but Ace didn't move in here after her death."

"Mr. Bolton didn't take in his grandchild?"

Marnie shook her head as she dropped another bombshell. "He didn't want to take in his bastard grandson. Ace's father wasn't in the picture either by the way."

I was stunned into silence. This story kept getting worse and worse. I was almost afraid to ask another question. "What happened to Ace then?"

"His mother's best friend took him in. Oh, I shouldn't be talking about this. I've already said too much. This isn't my story to tell."

"I appreciate you telling me this. I promise I won't tell anyone. It was a good thing that Ace had someone who stood up to take care of him after his mother died."

"Supposedly, Kiki had her own... interesting history."

I raised an eyebrow. "What was interesting about it? And what do you mean by 'had'?"

She froze for a moment, and I watched as her eyes darted around the room until they settled on me. "I've said way too much."

Before I could say anything further, I heard a door in the hallway open. I assumed Ace had arrived, and it was fitting that our conversation had ended when it did.

My suspicions were confirmed when he appeared in the doorway. He nodded at Marnie before turning to me.

I took in a deep breath as he stared at me without saying a word, his heated look warming my entire body.

"Come with me." Before I could respond, he turned around and left the doorway just as quickly as he entered.

His demand irritated me, but I didn't want to cause a scene in front of Marnie. I gave Marnie a small smile and followed Ace out of the room.

"What do you want?" I asked as he walked toward the stairs. He didn't give me an opportunity to catch up with him.

Ace halted his movements. I found myself staring at his back as I waited for him to speak. He looked at me over his left shoulder, the heated glare that I'd come to anticipate when he walked into a room.

"I'm going to fuck you."

My heart rate sped, and my body warmed at his words. I wanted him just as much as he wanted me. I watched as a lightbulb went off in his head and he picked me up and threw me over his shoulder as if I weighed nothing. I couldn't help but squeal in delight. The playfulness in my voice was something I hadn't heard in a long time, further increasing my excitement about what was to come.

"Harlow," he growled as he walked into my bedroom and closed the door behind him with his foot. He tossed me on the bed unceremoniously. The things I learned from Marnie were put on the back burner. It had been a few days since we'd had sex and time had only increased our need for one another.

I found him staring at my lips again and finally I'd had enough of not having any answers. "Why don't you kiss me?"

The question sounded almost desperate as it left my lips

and made me almost feel like a child. Is that a thing that people ask?

"It's not my thing," he said as he reached for my shirt. His answer confused me even more.

"What? I don't understand. Why?"

"Because it's too intimate."

I couldn't stop the hurt that rose to the surface. Why did I care that he didn't want to kiss me? I was only fulfilling my obligation for the money he paid to free me from Falcone's grasps.

Still the rejection was there and was bigger than I expected it to be. I couldn't do this right now.

"I don't want to do this, Ace."

He stopped his movements and looked at me.

A breath I didn't know I'd been holding left my lungs. It was then that I realized that I was wondering if I had once again been put into a situation where I was going to have to fight to not be raped.

The sternness in my voice made him freeze. He told me that I would never do what I didn't want to do and right now, I had no desire to have sex with him. This was far from your stereotypical relationship, but I wanted a level of trust that wasn't there.

He stared at me for a moment before he backed away and left through the door connecting our rooms.

27

ACE

"Do you mind if I join you?"

It was the next evening and I decided that I'd had enough of the silent treatment she was giving me. Harlow looked up from her position and nodded, making room for me on the couch.

We sat there in silence for a moment before I spoke. "I'm sorry for how I handled your question about kissing."

She rose up from her position on the couch and said, "I'm sorry too. I should have respected that it was a boundary that you had, but I took it as if it were an attack on me."

"It has nothing to do with you, I swear." I turned to look her in the eyes.

This was feeling too good to be true, and I knew it was.

Relaxing on the couch with Harlow was too domestic for my liking, yet I didn't try to leave like I did after we fucked. Being this close to her clouded my thoughts and made me want things I had no right to want.

Having her live here full-time was feeling more permanent and it was becoming an issue. We weren't in a relationship, nor was there any prospect of this turning into a fairy tale. I was deeply flawed, and I didn't want to drag her down into my shit either.

Yes, Harlow's life hadn't been easy by any means, but there was no way I was going to add to her struggles with some of mine. She didn't deserve it, but what I could admit to myself was that I couldn't get enough. It had started out with me seeing the scared young woman on a stage and thinking I could save her, and as a reward, I would get to have her in any way that I wanted. But now, I wanted to be with her always, much to the detriment of any work I needed to get done. Kingston and Gage had laid off their teasing on the last few calls that we had together. But I had a feeling that they noticed that I was still somewhat preoccupied, and that was a problem, given what I was trying to do.

Finding out more about Falcone and his dealings was the priority. I knew I was getting closer with the hints he'd dropped during our last meeting, but I still needed something more definite.

But this right here? Sitting with Harlow and doing absolutely nothing? This was the paradise I'd never expected to find.

"There's something I want to talk to you about."

Harlow moved her book to the coffee table and gave me her undivided attention. "Uh-oh. This sounds serious."

The last time I declared something like this it was about us not using condoms.

"What do you want to discuss?"

"How you came to be involved with Falcone."

"That story isn't all that interesting."

"Try me."

"An associate of mine knew that he was in the business of lending money fast, and I needed to bury my adoptive mother, so I went to him. Somehow along the way, the terms of the deal changed, and I ended up working at Bar 53."

How I wished that for her sake she hadn't gotten involved with the asshole.

THE NEXT DAY, I watched as Harlow did another lap in the pool, enjoying not only the way her body looked, but the way she moved through the water. It was hard to take my eyes off of her.

"Your car is here, Sir."

"Thanks, Anderson," I said as I walked around him and back up the stairs toward the front door. I buttoned my suit jacket and walked outside. I found the driver that I hired for the evening standing near the back door. He nodded as he opened the door and closed it behind me once I was seated.

I could have driven to my meeting, but I'd hired a driver because I didn't feel like driving through New York City traffic. I was glad that we'd finally found a time that worked for everyone that would allow us to be able to give Will a full debriefing of what I'd found.

One thought entered my mind that I couldn't seem to shake. Falcone seemed to be in a similar business as Kiki, but at least the world no longer had to deal with her terrorizing anyone, and as long as I walked this earth, I made a promise to kill her if someone didn't beat me to it. She'd done her part to steal the rest of my childhood after my mother died and she was made my legal guardian. And the old man who could have stopped it all did nothing. Instead, he gave me this house and a part of his fortune to continue running his business. And I'd gotten my revenge.

"What are you doing here?" That was the first thing out of Gage's mouth when he saw me.

"I got called to deliver this special package." I used my thumb to point back at the car. That was when his face registered that there was something in the back seat.

Gage walked over to the back seat, and I followed, making sure to stay a few feet behind him. When he opened the door, it didn't take long for me to smell the gasoline I'd poured all over the car door.

"Who greased some hands so that the charges against you were dropped?"

Kiki smiled. "What's the point in telling you? It's not like it's going to save my life anyway. Martin and Selena tried to make my life a living hell years ago after they kicked me out of their inner circle, but I persevered. I already got what I wanted: I made it so that you'll never forget me."

"You are sick. Even as you're about to die, you can't, in your good conscience, do something right. Ace?"

"Yeah?" I responded.

"Do you have anything that you want to say to her?"

I shook my head. "She and I had plenty to talk about on the way here."

"Then you do the honors." Gage rolled down the window a bit and then slammed the door of the car shut.

"The answer is closer than you think."

She'd barely got the words out before the fire in the car started getting to her and all Gage and I could hear were her screams. He and I stood there watching as the car burned. I pulled something out of my pocket to hand to him.

"Cigarette?"

"Nah, man, I don't smoke."

I looked at him, then at the cigarettes, and then back at him. "Yeah, I probably shouldn't either."

The temptation to light up was still there, but I refrained. My mother would be proud. I thought about my mother and how she thought that her best friend would have been the logical choice to be a guardian for her son once she'd succumbed to her disease. Not even her own flesh and blood was willing to come to her aid during her time of need.

I called Anderson and said, "In about two hours, arrange to have a car bring Harlow into the city. I'll send the address and an outfit for her to wear." It was time that we had a bit of fun in the city.

Soon, I was walking into Elevate, which was still somewhat quiet, given that it wasn't prime time yet. The party atmosphere that I'd seen on the few occasions that I came here, was nowhere to be found, but I knew that within an hour or so, the scenery here would do a one-eighty. I was the first to arrive and was brought to a table in the VIP area. No one else was here yet so I sat down and pulled out my phone to tie up a few loose ends before the meeting with Will.

"Can I get you something to drink?"

I looked at the server standing next to me. "I'll wait for everyone else to arrive."

With a slight nod, the server left me alone once more and my eyes were glued back to the device in my hand. Once I finished up what I needed to do, I double checked the plans that I'd made for Harlow and me and when I looked up, I found Kingston and Gage walking toward me.

"Will should be here shortly. Got stuck in traffic," Kingston said as they walked up.

"Or he's panicking about being in Cross territory now."

Both Kingston and I shook our heads at Gage as the two joined me at our table.

"Damien was going to join, but he had a prior engagement with his fiancée."

I nodded and all eyes turned to look at Will as he walked up to us with two bodyguards flanking him. He shook each of our hands and then took the remaining seat, whereas his guards backed away, but still within distance to do something if they thought there was a danger posed to his boss.

"You can speak freely here," Kingston said.

I looked at each of the men around the table and then spoke about all of the information that I'd found out about Falcone so far.

"You didn't mention Harlow," Gage said.

I rolled my eyes. "She has nothing to do with this conversation."

"That's not true at all," Gage said.

Will looked at me curiously. "Who is Harlow?"

"The woman that Ace bought at Falcone's auction," Kingston chimed in.

"You're foolish to get involved with Falcone, man." Will shook his head as he took a sip of his drink.

"Tell me something I don't already know. Look, I know what I'm doing, and you don't need to worry about it."

Will scoffed. "I'm not worried about who you're fucking, Ace. But you should be."

28

HARLOW

My fingers touched the phone screen once more, rereading the text message that I'd received from Ace a couple of hours ago now.

Ace: *We are going to Elevate tonight, Sweetness. Wear the outfit that I had sent to you. There will be a driver to pick you up.*

I wasn't expecting to come back to the city. Nor had I thought that I would be wearing this short, satin red dress or these matching high heels. The coat I had on covered most of it, but with enough leg showing, it was obvious that the outfit I had on was short.

Much like the color of my outfit, the effort that I put into my hair and makeup almost reminded me of when I was preparing to go on the auction block. But this felt different.

I wasn't holding my hands, a coping mechanism that I developed after hopping from home to home. There was no desire to do so because I didn't feel fear. At some point, I'd grown to trust Ace more than I was willing to admit out loud and it was only now that I'd realized it.

I checked myself in the rearview mirror just as the driver

looked up to see what I was doing. Instead of making eye contact, I turned to look out of the window. This moment reminded me of when I was driving to Falcone's home upstate, not knowing what my fate was going to be. Dread didn't follow me as I rode through the streets of New York City. Desire and excitement did.

Soon we pulled up to Elevate, a club I'd heard about through my work at Bar 53. I'd heard that it was supposed to be super exclusive and very hard to get into. So how had Ace gotten us in? I shook my head. Of course, Ace had no problems getting me into a sex club. I was slowly realizing it was foolish to doubt him. I waited for my driver to come around to my side of the car and open the door. As he was helping me out of the car, Ace appeared in front of me and the stunned look that I saw past his features was well worth the effort that I took to pull myself together. The best part of it was he hadn't seen this dress yet.

He took my hand from the driver and escorted me into the building. The first thing I was greeted with was the sounds of a Top 40 hit playing from the speakers. It wasn't as loud as I expected it to be, but if I was being honest given that it seemed as if we'd just walked onto the floor that contained a dance floor and bar.

Elevate was designed very sophisticatedly with black, gray, and gold colors. I looked around but didn't see anything that screamed sex club.

Ace chuckled next to me, before he leaned down to whisper in my ear, "Club is downstairs and you're going to need this to enter."

He handed me what looked to be a key that was designed to be old-fashioned but with a gold E on it. I palmed the key as he took my hand and led me through the crowd. It seemed as if he was familiar with the layout, which I found to be interesting.

"Did you want anything to eat or drink before we head down?"

I shook my head, my nerves slamming around my body as if they were trying to escape. I ate before I'd gotten into the car, and I was too nervous to have a drink although it might have calmed my nerves. Having a clear mind about tonight was important to me.

Ace led me to a door that was guarded by a man. He nodded at us, and Ace pulled out another key and held it up to the scanner. I followed suit and the guard opened the door which led to a set of stairs and a long hallway. Ace held my hand as I walked down the stairs, making sure that I didn't trip and led us over to a window where we needed to turn in our electronics, and I checked my coat. I could feel Ace's eyes burning a hole in me as he watched me take off my coat and hand it to the attendant. Once we had that sorted, Ace placed his hand on the small of my back and led me to a door on our left. He looked at me before he opened the door and allowed me to walk inside first.

My eyes scanned the room quickly, trying to take all of it in. The room was very dark, with candles providing the only light. I could make out the big bed in the center of the room.

"Look up," Ace said.

And that was when I saw it. The stars that were splayed out on the ceiling, giving the illusion of laying underneath them.

"How did this come about?"

"Visiting the club?" Ace said and I nodded. "My friends own the place."

"You didn't know if I would want to attend a sex club."

"I thought I would change our environment, but we don't need to experiment too much if you don't want to. And now I want to fuck you among the stars."

I'd grown used to him undressing me first, but this time, the fire in his eyes kept me firmly in place. I stared at him, watching as he removed his suit jacket, leaving him in a white button-down and black slacks.

I knew what he looked like naked, yet I couldn't help but be enticed as I watched his every movement.

He grabbed me in one quick motion. He turned me around so that my back was up against his chest. I couldn't tell if I was listening to the pounding of his heart in my ear or my own.

I held my breath as I felt his fingertips on my thighs. His big hands grabbed at the fabric of my dress and scrunched it up in his hands, exposing my thighs.

"Fuck, baby." His voice sounded raw against the shell of my ear.

I shivered as his breath tickled my ear and goose bumps appeared on my flesh. He bent down and attacked my neck, alternating between licking and lightly sucking on my skin. Ace slowly drew the dress up my body, the cool fabric increasing the sensations that I felt from his touch.

Once he lifted the dress over my head I heard him mutter a cuss word under his breath.

"You were naked under that?"

"Yeah," I said matter-of-factly. After all, my current state of undress spoke for itself.

A low growl came from his lips before he turned me around and backed me onto the bed. When I was lying on my back, I watched as he unbuttoned his shirt. I couldn't help but watch as his muscles moved and when he shed his shirt, I licked my lips without thinking about it. Soon he crawled up my body and our faces were only inches from one another.

"Was it your goal to be a tease?" he asked, the light ember in his gaze warming me.

I could have easily worn a thong or something under it but chose not to. Daring was the mood of the night for me. "No, I didn't want the lines from my underwear..."

My words trailed off as the heat in his eyes increased tenfold. Anything other than taking over everything completely was not an option. His lips were but a whisper away from mine and now I thought might finally be the time he would lean down and kiss me.

Hurt flashed in his eyes before the heat returned and his mouth was on my body. He grabbed my hair and pulled down on it, exposing more of my neck to his gaze. I felt my nipples harden under his gaze. He left light kisses from my neck down to my breasts. As his tongue swirled around my nipples, his hand found its way to my pussy. We both groaned when he discovered how wet I was.

He used his finger to tease me, refusing to go any further and I knew it was more than likely because of him discovering that I wasn't wearing anything underneath this dress.

"Please, Ace," I said, and my voice sounded desperate to my own ears, but the shame that I thought I would feel from begging wasn't there.

"Tell me what you want."

His question was simple, but my answer was more

complicated than that. Instead I chose to stick to the easy answer.

"I want you to fuck me, whether it's with your fingers or cock. I need it badly." The words rushed out of my mouth like a stock car speeding down a speedway.

"I could never deny you."

Before I could react to what he said, his finger plunged into my center and my gasp turned into moans when he didn't waste any time getting up to speed. When he added a second finger, it was as if my body took off like a rocket ship.

"Oh my—Fuck!" It was the only thing I could think to say as my hand reached around to land on his shoulders. My grip on him immediately tightened and before I could blink, I was screaming in relief as I came all over his fingers.

"Good girl." His motions didn't cease as he helped me ride out my orgasm. When my breathing slowed down, I watched him through half closed eyes as he took a step back from the bed and removed his pants and boxers. I couldn't help but stare at his cock while he briefly stroked himself as he stared at my body. Questions about whether I could move or not circled in my brain as I somehow found the energy to move.

When I did move, I made my way toward him, caught in a trance by the way his hand moved freely over his cock. My fingers have a mind of their own and I wrapped them around his dick and licked his head. He grabbed me by my hair, firmly but nowhere near enough to hurt me. He pulled my head back to look up at him.

"I'm not lasting if you continue to do that," he said gruffly. "Turn over. I want to see that pretty ass."

He let my hair go and I ended up on my knees with my

ass facing him. As he climbed onto the bed behind me, a sliver of anticipation began to build as I waited for him to make his move.

I expected him to touch me so that he could begin fucking me from behind, but that was not the case. Instead, I felt a slap on my ass. I moaned and turned to look at him over my shoulder.

"I love how much you love this, Sweetness."

I stopped moving when he said the word 'love'. I didn't expect Ace Bolton to love anything, but himself.

When he slapped my ass again, I pushed my thoughts of anything but this experience away and got a chance to enjoy the warm feeling that not only covered my ass but spread across my whole body. When he slapped my ass for the third time, he took his time massaging the spot he hit before I felt his cock moving across my ass.

"Please," I said as I waited impatiently for him to put us both on the path to ecstasy.

I felt the head of his cock at my entrance just before he sank himself into my body, inch by inch. My fingers gripped the sheets on the bed as he slowly began moving inside of me. He readjusted slightly and it was as if a lightning bolt went off inside of him. His strokes became deeper, slowly driving my mind and body to another dimension. The angle that he was fucking me was potent, addictive in nature and I knew I would never get enough of this.

My orgasm hit me unexpectedly. I screamed and professed my love to anything and everything, but Ace kept fucking me like he was on a mission. A low moan grew into a louder groan when he too reached his climax. It was easy to tell that we were both spent as he collapsed on top of me briefly before rolling over to his side.

I only flipped my body over when I heard him leave the bed and soon he returned with a damp washcloth in hand. I gazed up at the stars as he wiped a cloth between my legs, and I watched as he gently cleaned me up. This was a complete change from the first time we'd had sex together. As he took care of me afterward, I felt loved. I couldn't remember the last time that I'd felt this way. But with every good thing in my life must come to an end as I remembered how he purposefully avoided my lips. I should ask him why, but for some reason, I was afraid to know the answer. The mood was further dampened by Ace's words from when we first met.

There will never be anything more to this than just sex.

His words rang in my head like a warning siren before an impending crash.

"Come on, we have to get dressed to leave."

"Where are we going? Back to your place?"

"To the penthouse suite at the Olympus Hotel. We'll be staying there for a couple of days."

My eyes widened as I rose to look at Ace's face. "Why are we staying in a hotel?"

Going back to Ace's home made more sense to me even though it was quite far from where we currently were. Staying in the same room with him tonight would be an entirely new experience, one that I had wondered about every night when I thought he might sneak into my room.

29

ACE

Staying in the same room let alone the same bed as Harlow was a mistake. This was supposed to be a temporary thing, but I could feel her slowly becoming ingrained in my life. There was no way I was pulling her into my shit. It was part of the reason why I'd taken refuge in the living room. The other reason was because a memory of mine decided to run wild and I didn't want to disturb Harlow any further.

Watching Kiki Hastings waltz out of jail like she was the belle of the ball felt like being punched in the gut by an MMA fighter. But this? This right here? Trounced any feelings I had that day. Because I was going to end this shit once and for all.

Her pleading in the background made me grin. Hearing her cry in the back seat, weeping for her life, fueled my joy. Her fear about what might happen to her made my grin widen. It sounded sadistic, even in my own head, but I didn't give a fuck. It was about time she paid for what she did. I didn't know how many men or women, girls or boys, she'd hurt over the years, but I knew there was no way that she would be able to do it anymore. Tonight would be putting an end to a chapter in my life.

She'd put a roof over my head and food in my belly when I was at my most vulnerable but took way more than she'd saved. Memories of her forcing me to kiss her every opportunity she got rose to the surface, and the nights she came into my room to "play with me" were thrown into the fire with her. She said it was all because I owed her after my mother died and she didn't have to take me in.

She even invited some of her friends to watch us in the act.

My mother had trusted her to take care of me because her own father wanted nothing to do with us.

I remember rejecting her one night and her shouting, "Do I have to remind you who I am? I could toss you out on the street right now and no one would give a shit."

She was right, or at least that was what I was made to believe. When the Cross family had found out what I'd been through, I knew guilt played a huge role in how they treated me with kid gloves over the years, and over time, we'd all moved on.

And then there was the time that my grandfather finally acknowledged me, once I was almost of age, all because he knew he needed to get an heir into place that would keep his businesses alive long after he was dead.

That was all that mattered to him, and I tossed those memories into the car as well. He could also go up in smoke with her for all I cared.

While I watched her burn to death in the car with Gage, my face remained stoic, taking it all in. Relief should have flowed through my veins, but I felt nothing.

The sound of my cell phone vibrating on the coffee table brought me out of my thoughts of Kiki. I should head back to bed because of how late it was.

Harlow and I got back from Elevate a couple of hours ago, just after midnight. We stayed longer than originally planned, but I couldn't get enough of her, and she was insatiable. When I opened the door to the penthouse suite of the Olympus Hotel, I carried Harlow across the threshold, tossed a shirt that was meant for me on her, and laid her down in the bed where I thought she could sleep peacefully. My racing thoughts stopped me from doing the same.

I looked down at the phone and found a message from Kingston. What the hell was he doing up this late?

Kingston: *Falcone has been asking questions.*

Me: *About?*

Kingston: *You. Could be trying to figure out whether doing business with you is worth it.*

That was a good development. I decided to reach out to him in the morning to talk at the very least. I grabbed the phone, turned it on silent, and walked back into the bedroom. Harlow's face was partially covered by her hair, making her appear slightly younger than her years. In her sleep, she looked more peaceful, as if the troubles in her world were sitting right on her doorstep, ready to slam into her as soon as she woke up.

It was then I noticed a scar on her shoulder. As if she knew I was staring at her while she was asleep, Harlow turned over, blocking my view of the scar. I couldn't help but wonder how it had gotten there. Was it a childhood injury? Or something more recent? I hadn't noticed her favoring that arm so maybe it was from something that happened long ago.

In any case, none of that would be getting answered right now, so I walked over to the other side of the bed and made sure that both Harlow and I were covered by the blanket before pulling her into my arms gently and falling asleep.

30

HARLOW

I woke up and found the moon creeping in through the blinds of the window. It took me a second to realize where I was. At some point during the night, Ace had pulled me into his arms, and I was currently laying on his chest, enjoying the sound of his heart beating in my ear. A part of me wanted to wake him up so we could go another round, but we both needed our rest so maybe it was best to fall back to sleep and enjoy the feeling of being in his arms for as long as I could.

To put myself back to sleep, I lightly ran my finger up and down his chest, enjoying the feel of his chest hair beneath my fingertip. And then my whole world shifted.

Before I could recognize what was happening, I was on my back with Ace hovering over me, my wrists pinned down by his hands.

"What the hell?" I yelled, but from what I could see of Ace's facial expression in the moonlight, my voice hadn't registered. Fear crawled up my spine at what he might do next. "Ace! You're hurting my wrists. Let me go!"

It was then that he seemed to hear me. He loosened his grip and then let go just before he rolled over onto his back. I didn't realize how hard I was breathing until I heard myself trying to catch my breath.

"What was that all about?" I asked between my labored breathing. For a split second, I wondered if he might have moved his hands so that he could wrap them around my throat, much like Ian had done.

"It was nothing, Harlow. Go back to sleep." Ace moved so that he could sit up on the edge of the bed. From where I lay, I could see that he was running both hands over his face. Then he stood up.

"I want to talk about this. Something had to have caused you to react that way even in sleep. I want to help you." I'd had plenty of nightmares throughout my life to recognize that sign. What had happened to him to cause such a reaction?

"Just go back to sleep. I'm sorry all of this happened." With that, he walked out of the room, leaving me alone in the bed.

That was easier said than done and the harshness of his voice had me wondering if he was referring to more than just what had happened mere minutes ago.

THE SUNLIGHT CARESSED my face like a warm blanket, making me want to further bury myself into the warm cocoon that kept the rest of me warm. If the bed in Ace's guest room was the best bed I'd ever laid my head down on, this bed came in second. I didn't want to leave, but something else was forcing me awake. The smell of bacon forced me up and my stomach growled soon after.

I threw the blankets off me and found myself dressed in a shirt that was too big for me. It was reminiscent of one that Ace had worn. How I'd gotten into the shirt was a bit fuzzy, but him grabbing me last night wasn't.

I tried to shake the feeling that came over me as I found a robe draped over a chair on the other side of the bedroom. As I was tying the robe over my body, memories of the night before replayed in my mind. I remembered Ace carrying me into the suite and then helping me out of the clothes I wore to Elevate. After dressing me once more, I remembered him tucking me in and brushing my hair before leaving the room.

I turned to look at the bed and it was obvious that he had come back to bed at some point, but when, I had no idea. Would he want to talk about what happened between us last night? From our evening at Elevate to him pinning me down, potentially just moments from attacking me, the range of emotions that we'd gone through last night felt like we were on a roller coaster. With a deep breath, I swung the bedroom door open and walked out into what I soon discovered was the living room and kitchen area.

My mouth dropped open at what was laid out before me. A buffet of breakfast foods, including the bacon that I smelled while in the bedroom. Included with the food was a bottle of chilled champagne and a pitcher of orange juice. My eyes darted around the room to confirm that Ace wasn't there.

"Ace?" I called out but heard nothing in response. Where could he be?

I took an opportunity to study the room before me. Last night, I was half asleep when I entered the space, and it was clear that I'd missed a lot of what this room had to offer. My eyes ended up back on the food in front of me.

"You're awake."

I looked up and found Ace walking out of another room that was connected to the suite. He was wearing slacks and a white button-down, which was basically his uniform when doing something related to work. It looked cleaned and crisp though, so I assumed he'd had clothes delivered to the hotel at some point.

"I am. Where did you come from?"

"There's an office space on the other end of the suite. I had a quick phone call that I'll fill you in on once we sit down and eat. You have to be starving after last night."

As if on cue, my stomach growled again, and I shrugged as Ace smirked. He led me to the table and once I was seated, I took in the food across the table. There was fruit, eggs Benedict, bacon, and a host of other foods. It was enough to feed more than two people.

"I didn't know what you were in the mood for, so I ordered it all."

His thinking about what I would have wanted to eat instead of choosing to order for me or expecting me to eat whatever he was eating made my heart warm. He made our mimosas as I served myself and I waited until he had food on his plate before I started eating my meal.

"How are you feeling?"

I waited a second to respond to give myself a chance to swallow the food in my mouth. "Fine?"

"After the marathon last night turned into, I wanted to check in."

So he was going to focus on Elevate, not what happened

after. I didn't want to push him, especially if it was something very painful, so I buried the questions I had in my mind. After all, I had my own secrets as well. I smiled back at him, although I wasn't feeling particularly happy. "I'm fine. Much more relaxed I have to say."

"Good. Good."

I took a sip of the mimosa and closed my eyes, enjoying the taste of the drink. It also provided some liquor courage for the comment I wanted to make. I waited a beat to see if he would say something else. When he didn't, I spoke. "I want to go back. I'm interested in experiencing more of the rooms."

Ace's gaze met mine and I saw something flash across them, almost lightening them in a way before it was tucked away in the back of his mind, much like he kept all of his thoughts under lock and key.

He cleared his throat before he spoke. "Today is going to be a busy day."

"Really? Why's that?"

"I have a few things that I want to take you to around the city, but I do have a quick meeting that I must attend this evening."

I raised an eyebrow at him because this was the first time he was letting me in on any sort of business dealings he was involved with. "Do I know with whom?"

"You do. It's Falcone, but I'll go and do that by myself later. First, whatever you want to do today while we are here in New York City."

I weighed the events that he laid out in front of me. "I want to go with you to see him."

"No."

I tightened my grip on the fork in my hand. "I want to go see him."

"The business he and I have to discuss has nothing to do with you and could be dangerous. You will stay here."

"Do you think I'll miss the opportunity to show him that he will never have control over me again?"

This time, Ace smirked at me. "You make a pretty fair point, and I don't think he'd be expecting you to be there, which might work in my favor... Fine. You may come along, but if I tell you to do something, do it. It might be for your own safety."

"Or is it you getting off on telling me what to do?"

This time, his hardened stare was the only answer I received in return, and I wondered if my choice to go with him was now a big mistake.

31

ACE

"I can't believe you brought me here!" Harlow exclaimed as she tried to exit the car as quickly as possible. The heels she decided to wear today hindered her, making her appear more clumsy than normal. Once we'd safely gotten her out of the car, we both walked into The Attic, a bookstore near her alma mater, New York University. Given her love of books and the proximity of the store to her college, I made an educated guess that she would want to visit. I was right.

Her energy was infectious as she walked up and down the aisles, taking in the books and the place that she hadn't been to in a while. "This place made me want to own my own bookshop one day."

That didn't shock me. "Owning a bookshop would be perfect for you."

She beamed at me, and my heart skipped a beat. I pushed the feeling away as I trailed behind her, watching as she picked up books to purchase.

Deep down, I knew that she would one day own a bookshop because based on the time that I'd known her and the research that we'd uncovered about her, she also pushed herself to persevere no matter what hurdle was thrown in her way. What I also knew was that I wouldn't be there to watch her achieve her dream.

She had her whole life to live and it was foolish of me to think that she would eventually want to be saddled with an older man who was still fighting the demons that haunted him as a child. Could I blame her after I pinned her down in the bed last night because I thought she was trying to hurt me in my dreamlike state? No, I couldn't. But for now, I'd enjoy watching how happy she was in this moment.

We spent about an hour in The Attic and once her books were paid for, we got back into the car I hired to take us to the final stop on this journey. We were a block away from Bar 53 and I noticed Harlow was cupping one hand in the other. I didn't like that going back to her old job made her nervous. I grabbed her hand before giving it a gentle squeeze. She looked over at me and gave me a small smile before turning to look back out the window. For some reason, I was surprised she didn't remove her hand from mine. I couldn't remember the last time that my touch had provided comfort to someone outside of the bedroom, but it felt good.

Nice.

Warm.

Love.

It took everything in me not to snatch my hand away when that thought entered my mind. Thankfully, the driver I hired pulled to a stop across the street from Bar 53 since there were no parking spots in front of the bar. Instead of waiting for the driver, I got out of the car and helped Harlow exit as well. I couldn't help but glance at her as she stepped out of the vehicle. She opted for one of the black business casual dresses that I'd had sent to the penthouse with nude pumps, making her legs look a thousand miles long. I couldn't help but notice how well we matched one another.

I mentioned my name to the host at the front desk and we walked into the bar area before we were stopped by a shout.

"Harlow!"

Both Harlow and I turned around and I found a dark-haired woman running toward Harlow. I put my hand up to stop her from getting too close and Harlow placed her hand over mine. With a small nod, she told me that there was more than met the eye when it came to her relationship with the woman in front of us.

"Emma, how are you?"

So that was the woman's name.

"What do you mean, how am I? How are you?" She raised her voice slightly and glanced over at me.

"I'm fine."

"Happy?" She tried to whisper this question but failed.

"Yes," Harlow answered without hesitation, but I knew she was lying.

How could she be happy living in the middle of nowhere after being snatched from everything she'd known?

Emma and Harlow chatted quietly for a few more moments before I cleared my throat. We had a meeting to get to and I didn't want to stay here longer than necessary.

Harlow reached over and hugged Emma, before giving her a big smile that didn't quite reach her eyes. She then walked over to me and together we followed the host down the stairs to Falcone's office.

My thoughts shifted once we were in the basement and were just feet from Falcone's door. Nothing looked different including the guard that usually stood in front of Falcone's door. He nodded as he opened the door for us. I wasn't surprised to find Falcone sitting behind his desk, but I was shocked to find Ian in the room.

"Mr. Bolton, welcome. And I see you've brought a guest."

"It seems that you've done the same."

Falcone reached over and shook my hand and Ian had no issue doing the same. I noticed that while Falcone looked somewhat indifferent to Harlow being in the room, Ian's reaction was the exact opposite. There was no hiding the anger in his eyes, and it was fixated on Harlow. There was something that I didn't know about this scenario, but I was going to find out.

"Please have a seat."

At Falcone's invitation, Harlow and I sat in the seats situated at the front of his desk. Ian kept his positioning near his boss while Falcone took his seat once more.

"I didn't suspect that I would be talking about business... in front of an audience."

I shrugged nonchalantly. "I figured you would want to know how things were going between Harlow and me anyway. After all, the deal I made with you is why she is with me anyway."

Out of the corner of my eye, I saw Harlow stiffen next to me. The pang I felt at making her feel uncomfortable hurt me, but I was able to mask those feelings from my face. I shouldn't have allowed her to come with me. I couldn't afford to have the distraction. Falcone might not think of her as being a way to get to me because he knew about our agreement, but someone else might think that taking her out would be the quickest way to attack me. And I couldn't afford to have her death on my conscience. I needed to cut the cord before this got too deep and that started with us not having sex anymore. The sex part of our relationship had muddled shit up and things would be better if she went back to hating me, but I knew that this would have to be dealt with when we got back to my home.

"Ian knows about the things that I do, and I wouldn't be surprised if our dear Harlow here didn't pick up on a thing or two while working here."

"So you have no issue with talking about these things in front of her?"

This time it was Falcone's turn to shrug. "My business practices clearly aren't a secret between the four of us given what has taken place."

He had a good point. After all, he let me purchase Harlow out of a loan that he'd had over her.

"Go on," I said as Harlow shifted in her seat again. My gaze landed on Ian, who I found staring at Harlow. I cleared my throat loudly and both he and Falcone looked at me. With my glare fixated on him, Ian looked away.

"I'm in the process of bringing some of my... businesses to Midtown. Drug trafficking, arms dealing, and maybe opening up a brothel where more auctions could take place. Local police and politicians have all been taken care of so that is not a concern. If you're interested, Bolton, I'm more than willing to let you in. You could make even more billions."

"Isn't that Will DePalma's territory?" It was a question that I didn't need to ask because I knew it was. I just wanted to get him to admit it out loud.

"That is what he thinks. The foundation for my takeover has already been set, so it's just a matter of time. Will has lost control of his organization and that's all I'm willing to say about him."

This is what I'd wanted to know. This was the information I needed to tell Will.

"So what do you say, Ace? Are you in?"

I let his words hang as something else had dawned on me: putting together what might have happened between Ian and Harlow. "I'm still going to need some time to see how we might be able to... entice you on our end."

I knew what resources I had at my disposal and could easily spout them off, but I had no intention of doing any business with him even if my grandfather thought it would be a wise decision.

"That's fine. I'll follow up at a later date." He stood up once more and Harlow and I did the same. He shook my hand and then turned to Ian. "Why don't you show them to the front door?"

With a slight nod, Ian walked around and didn't acknowledge me because his eyes were trained on Harlow. I cleared my throat and then he looked at me, as if he'd just noticed I was standing there. Fear flashed in his eyes before he walked to the door. Had he thought that I wouldn't acknowledge his behavior toward her?

I waited until Ian had walked us all the way to the front door and before he could leave us to go on our merry way, I said, "I'd like a word with you."

He looked at me, but his expression remained blank as he held the door open for Harlow and me and then he followed suit. When he was standing in front of me, his eyes darted between me and looking around, maybe trying to find a witness or someone to help him if I decided to fuck him up on a public street. I saw the driver that I hired for this trip and decided to make this last bit quick.

Instead, I leaned over and said, "I don't know everything about what happened between you and Harlow, but if you so much as look in her direction again, I will make sure your body is never found."

Harlow grabbed my arm and squeezed. The fear that I saw in Ian's eyes earlier was back, but he quickly masked it. I had no doubt that he would go back and tell Falcone what had just happened between us. Now that I had my answer about what Falcone was doing, I had enough information to tell Will and warn him about what I knew of Falcone's game plan.

Ian was left looking at me, speechless by my statement. Good. May he heed that warning and not end up a dead man. I turned around and lightly pulled Harlow so that she was standing in front of me. I glanced over my shoulder at Ian as we walked to the town car and found him staring at us as we left.

I'd settled a score for Harlow that should provide some relief for her when I told her that any relations between us were over.

32

HARLOW

"Harlow, thanks for coming to my office. We need to talk about something."

"What's that?" I stared at him, noticing the seriousness of his expression. It was the evening after the Falcone meeting, and I couldn't say I was surprised to find that Ace wanted to talk. After he'd stalled Falcone enough to not give him a straight answer on whether he wanted to join him in his new ventures, the mood between him and me had changed. He grew quieter than what had become our norm and it had put me on high alert. But I wasn't willing to ask him about it because I was afraid of the answer.

"We need to stop doing this."

I felt my eyes widen and my mouth dropped open. "Stop doing what? Whatever this is?" I asked as I gestured between the two of us. When he didn't deny what I said, I continued. "I'm filling out the obligations that we agreed to."

"I know, and I'm telling you that you no longer have to do this. You can stay here until the three months are up, but we'll pretend as if we are nothing more than roommates who barely see one another. I'll have Anderson switch your bedroom."

"Wait, what? Do I have a say in any of this?"

"No. This is the only way it can be between us."

I stared at him in disbelief before I recovered. "No."

"What do you mean, no?"

"I'm not going to let you do this to us."

"Harlow, there is no 'us'. You have no choice in this matter."

I couldn't believe myself. I did what I said I wouldn't do. My emotions had been played like a fiddle, and I was left feeling like such a fool. But he warned me that this would happen, and I didn't listen because I thought that there was no way I would fall for someone who bid on me at an auction. Yet here I was.

The coldness that I felt from him was like a slap in the face, but I refused to let him see me cry. Even though that was all I wanted to do.

"Do you understand?" The simple words cut through me like a knife.

"Yes, I do."

"You may leave."

I turned and walked away after being dismissed from his office and what felt like his life. Only when I closed the door behind me did I finally let the tears that threatened to fall go.

I told myself I wouldn't fall in love with him. Yet here I was spinning from the reality that had slapped me in the face: Ace didn't love me. I was convinced that he couldn't ever love anyone.

There was no way I could stay here any longer. Living in the same home as him would be too painful. Not to mention, this place wasn't mine and never had been. Hell, I'd even argue it wasn't Ace's either given how much he didn't seem to give a shit about making anything here his.

It was as if he was just passing through life, without a care in the world unless it pertained to him doing something that required him to leave the house or fucking me.

When we came together at night it was magic, but it bothered me more than I cared to admit that he wouldn't kiss my lips. I'd watched him stare at them with longing, but he never gave in to temptation.

Although it was a boundary of his, the fact that he didn't kiss me once still hurt.

I didn't realize how much I longed for that connection until I had anything but. And I deserved better. I couldn't fake my feelings for him or stand to be around him for the remainder of the time left on the deal with Falcone. Seeing him when he was around hurt too much.

He was right. I would never be the same. Ace had ruined me unapologetically, and he warned me that he would the first time we fucked. And I didn't listen to him.

With a shaky breath, I grabbed my phone and called the only person I could trust in this predicament.

"Hello?"

"Hey, Emma. I'm going to need your help."

I WALKED over to the bathroom and stared at myself in the mirror. The evidence of my tears was still there as I looked at my blotched face in the mirror. I wiped at the wetness that was still present on my face. I sucked in several deep breaths to try to calm myself down. Once my emotions were more stable, I found some paper and a pen and wrote a letter to him that I would leave for him once I was gone.

Ace,

I couldn't stay with you any longer. I know writing this letter is taking the cowardly way out, but I knew saying these words to you in person would lead to more heartache than I could bear to show.

The truth is that I can't stay in that house another moment. It has gotten to the point where it pains me to be near you. You are still keeping things from me, no matter how close I'd thought we'd gotten. It hurts, and I deserve better.

I know that this is breaking the agreement we shared, and I understand that. I'll figure out a way to pay back Falcone myself.

Harlow

"Do you need anything else before you head out?"

I shook my head, not trusting myself to speak. Anderson gave me a slight nod before I walked across the threshold, and he closed the door behind me. More than likely forever.

It took me a couple of days to plan for my escape, but it hadn't been that difficult. Ace wanted nothing to do with me so that made things so much easier, and I was leaving with even less stuff than what I came with, but it was all that I could manage to pack without arousing suspicion.

I sat in the car and looked back at the place that had been my protection in a way. It had protected me from Falcone's wrath and given me somewhere to escape that got me away from Ian after he'd attacked me.

It had become my temporary home and now, I had to flee.

I played with the bracelet he gave me. It was a beautiful piece but meant nothing.

I'd parked in front of the bookstore and stared up at it, knowing that this would more than likely be the last time that I saw it. It was early enough in the day that it was easy to find parking and I was grateful for that.

Tears welled up in my eyes as I thought about what I'd left behind to get to this point. When I saw Emma pull into a parking spot on the opposite side of the street, I wiped my eyes, grabbed my bag that had everything I owned, and exited the car. I locked the car and walked over to Emma's.

She rolled down the passenger side window and unlocked her car doors with a small smile. "Long time no see."

I placed my bag in the back seat and closed the door. I walked around to talk to her through the passenger side window. "It's only been a few days. Thanks so much for driving up here to get me."

"Of course. You know I would do anything for you."

I glanced down at the bracelet on my wrist and took it off. "Here, take this. I know it might not be much, but I rather not have anything that reminds me of Ace anyway. Hopefully that could be some sort of payment..."

"No, Harlow. I won't—"

"There's one last thing I need to do, and it will just take me a minute. Be right back."

I watched Emma nod and I walked away, not giving her a chance to debate with me further. Chances are it would come up again on our ride anyway. I ran into the bookstore and found Chanel.

"Harlow, happy to see you again." Her cheerful grin darkened as she studied my face. "What's wrong?"

I sniffled quietly to myself and said, "Nothing. Um, would you be willing to do me a favor?"

Chanel looked a little uneasy. "Sure? What do you want me to do?"

"Can you give this to Anderson or Ace?" I handed her the set of car keys that I had, and she looked at them as if they were a foreign object. "I appreciate it, but I have to go."

"Harlow, wait," she said, but I didn't listen. Every minute that ticked by was crucial. I needed to get out of town as fast as possible. I gave her a small wave before I jogged to the door.

I knew that Ace had some sort of tracker on the car, so he'd be able to track it down. This time, however, I wouldn't be anywhere near it.

33

ACE

"I'm glad you were able to accommodate me on such short notice," Parker Townsend said as he took a seat in front of me. What I didn't tell him was I decided to take this meeting in my office in the city because it gave me an opportunity to get away from all things Harlow that seemed to follow me around my home.

"No problem. I have to say, I've been waiting for you to reach out."

"I apologize for how long it took for this to happen. I had some business to handle involving the Chevaliers that I needed to take care of before I came to you, but I promise this will be quick because I mostly came here to drop something off."

I wanted to ask what that was all about, but I knew he wouldn't tell me. As chairman of the Chevaliers, he might have access to even more information than the Cross family.

"I think what is in this envelope will help you clear up a lot of confusion that you have about your grandfather."

"How do you—" I stopped my train of thought. Of course

he had some information on my grandfather. With him also being a member of the Chevaliers, it made sense.

"I can see in your eyes that you're questioning how I have this information. Word gets around and you weren't exactly being quiet about what you were doing."

That was true and had been done on purpose. He handed a manila envelope to me that I took with an eyebrow raised.

"You're going to be very interested in what is in that envelope. I'll be in touch."

He left my office as quickly as he came, and I was left in a bigger state of confusion than I'd been when he entered. I debated opening the envelope here, but I couldn't. I needed to be home to do the big reveal.

Instead of waiting around for a conference call that was supposed to take place today, I decided to take the call from my car. It would allow me to beat some of the traffic back home and would stop me from thinking of the manilla envelope that Parker gave me before he left my office. I glanced at it sitting in my passenger seat, almost begging me to open it right now, but I needed to concentrate on driving and on what my team was reporting on this call. As I was pulling up to my home and wrapping up the conference call, I saw that Kingston was calling.

"We'll have follow-up questions about the report that was given, I'm sure but good work. I have another call to catch, so this call is over."

I walked into my home as people were saying their good-byes. Anderson wasn't standing at the front door, which was a bit odd, but I didn't have time to think about it. When I reached my office, I hung up and answered Kingston's call.

"About time you called me back. I've been trying to set up

a call or meeting with Will to tell him what I know and haven't been able to reach him and then you ghosted me."

"I'm not sure what is up with Will, but I'll see what I can find out from him after we get off the phone. "

"Good although any conversation with him would be quick. I'd be confirming what he thought."

"I need to tell—" Kingston stopped talking. "Are you serious?"

"Yep. His intel was correct."

"Interesting, but all of that needs to be put on the back burner right now, although it is connected to what I'm about to say."

"Well... speak," I said.

"Falcone found out that the reason why you were at his party was because you were trying to find out information for Will DePalma. And he's pissed."

I knew it was only a matter of time. Falcone wasn't a complete idiot. People talked, and to be honest, I was surprised that it took this long for anyone to realize that I had gone to the auction with ulterior motives. And to be fair, I didn't care if he came after me. What wasn't okay was that I had brought Harlow into this shitstorm.

With Kingston calling to confirm, I wasn't surprised.

"None of this is shocking."

"Well, how about this? Her connection to Falcone might run deeper than we expected. Her friend Emma?"

"Yeah?" I recalled the dark-haired woman that had ambushed Harlow when we'd arrived at Bar 53.

"We couldn't find shit on her either. Everyone who works at Bar 53 supposedly owes Falcone something. There are only two people who don't. Ian, who paid his loan off and moved up to a management role, if you want to call it that, and Emma."

"So what the hell is Emma doing there?"

"Your guess is as good as mine, but until we find out more, she shouldn't be trusted. Which leads me to my next point. You know Falcone's going to come after Harlow, right? Whatever deal you had to get her has been thrown out the window."

"I know." Although we couldn't be anything more than what we were. She deserved to have the fullest protection that I could provide, because Falcone now had a double hardon for her because of me. Not to mention this probably only enraged is lackey, Ian, further.

"Do you need some of my men to come out and help guard?"

"I wouldn't say no to extra help, but I know how to protect what's mine."

"Yours?"

The words slipped out, bypassing any filter that I might have had to keep my feelings to myself. I didn't really give a shit if he knew anyway.

"Look, we need to prepare for anything this fucker might bring. I'll call you back if I hear anything and I suspect that you'll do the same."

"Damn right."

With that, I hung up and was getting ready to send Anderson a message when there was a knock on my door.

"Come in."

The door opened and Anderson appeared. "She's gone, Sir. Chanel called and said that she left your car in front of her bookstore."

When he uttered those words, I was anything but surprised.

I'd witnessed how she'd pulled away from me almost immediately, and while it hurt, it was what I thought I deserved. And she and I both knew that she was excellent at running away and doing her best to disappear.

"She left this behind." He placed the smartphone, letter, and credit card on my desk before walking back over to the door.

"Thank you," I said, and Anderson dismissed himself. I flipped the credit card between my fingers as I read the letter before throwing it down on the desk so hard that it bounced and fell to the ground. Before it fell, it landed on the manila envelope that Parker had given to me.

Why was I upset? After all, this was what I wanted.

The bracelet that she wore told me exactly where she was and when. Turned out that my instinct to outfit it quickly with a tracker before giving it to her was the right one.

I picked up my cell phone and tapped on the name I wanted to call.

"Hello? What happened that you needed to call me back this fast?"

"Harlow is gone."

"Wait a minute, she's what?"

I couldn't believe the words myself, but none of this deserved to be a shock. I'd pushed her away, so it made sense that she left. What I didn't expect to feel was this pang that I couldn't explain.

"Harlow is gone and I'm going to find her."

THANK YOU FOR READING! The next book in the series, The Billionaire's Possession, will be released in Spring 2022.

WANT to join the discussion about the The Ruthless Billionaire Trilogy? Click HERE to join my Reader Group on Facebook.

PLEASE JOIN my newsletter to find out the latest about the The Ruthless Billionaire Trilogy and my other books!

ABOUT THE AUTHOR

Bri loves a good romance, especially ones that involve a hot anti-hero. That is why she likes to turn the dial up a notch with her own writing. Her Broken Cross series is her debut dark romance series.

She spends most of her time hanging out with her family, plotting her next novel, or reading books by other romance authors.

briblackwood.com

ALSO BY BRI BLACKWOOD

Broken Cross Series

Sinners Empire (Prequel)

Savage Empire

Scarred Empire

Steel Empire

Shadow Empire

Secret Empire

Stolen Empire

The Broken Cross Series Box Set: Books 1-3

The Ruthless Billionaire Trilogy

The Billionaire's Auction

The Billionaire's Possession

Brentson University Series

Devious Game